WANTON WOMEN

WANTON WOMEN

A collection of twenty erotic stories

Edited by Miranda Forbes

Published by Xcite Books Ltd – 2011
ISBN 9781907761683

Printed and bound in the UK

Cover design by Madamadari

Contents

Tango
by Alcamia Payne

When she split up from David, Sophie decided to find herself.

She'd wanted to learn to tango but David had told her she had no rhythm and she was as bad at dancing as she was inept at sex. For that reason Sophie, who fucked herself privately, also became a secret dancer, and danced privately in front of her cheval mirror.

Sophie wasn't quite certain what she wanted from sex any more, but she knew she needed it to be soft and sensual and packaged up in the haunting rhythms of the South American beat.

She didn't want harsh men's fingers buried in her sex – she wanted a sensual moving finger. She'd decided it might be nice to be fucked by a woman's fingers to the beat of the tango.

The old jazz club which was situated up a quiet backstreet was small, but because of this the syrupy seductive atmosphere was so thick and condensed, the vibe clung to her like treacle, and made her think of thick rich sex. There was nothing like salsa and tango and the odours of warm bodies, oozing perfumes and sex juices to turn Sophie on. She curled up in a corner and, as the music beat its sexual tattoo and she was squeezed within a warm glove of pleasure, the fingers of the erotic metaphorical tango glove, stroked her with an orgasmic serenade, eventually culminating in a series of satisfying, hip-rocking pulses.

After this she felt satiated and began to observe the dancers. Sophie easily lost herself in them, slipping inside their skins as she tried them on like items of clothing. There was always one dancer in particular who captivated her. It could be the fluidity of the movements, the tilt of the pelvis or the aggressive stance.

At midnight the dancefloor was full, since like moths to a flame, the shadows that had earlier clung around the fringes had by now gravitated towards its stage. Here they moved tirelessly like curious clockwork toys, as they engaged in dance sex – a secret language of thrusts and rotations, fierce interlocking limbs and caresses.

A couple swirled past Sophie, the woman's face a mask of erotic appreciation. She was not beautiful but she possessed a simmering sex which was rippling beneath the surface and trapped within her dancer's skin.

Sophie watched the man grind his groin into the fabulously orgasmic-looking woman and she wondered how the cock felt, as he spun her away from him in the vicious tango and snapped her back, hips grinding, legs apart, the expression one of a circumspect "Eat me", and all said with eyes and body.

The exotic men were stunning. Here was a smörgåsbord of sexual delicacies. She adored the heavy-lidded, long-lashed eyes which watched you with predatory intent. Engage them with your glance and there they were for the taking, sexual men saturated by tango and earthy beats who had become sex because of it. Sophie had travelled widely; she was a beautiful and intelligent girl, everyone said so, and she could have had such a man if she'd wanted him. But, she knew even he would not awaken her unless he was feminine. This point had angered her last boyfriend, David. He couldn't stand her love for feminine men. This craving inside her for the feminine and her reticence for his penile sex, unnerved him and he'd told her she was frigid and had a plug of ice between her legs. This enraged Sophie, who knew – yes, *knew* – she was passionate.

A striking man was watching her from a barstool. He had high angular cheekbones, thick black hair cut in an asymmetric style, falling forward in a fringe over dark-kohled gypsy eyes, and his legs in his tailored pants were slim and elegant and offset by an extremely narrow waist. It was the whorish slash of carmine lipstick on the androgynous face though, which

2

sealed her lust and made it percolate within her; hot and steamy and bubbling up.

For an instant Sophie began to climb the ladder of arousal, shivering with desire. She could imagine exciting sexual things about this man and they were intensely violent.

Her gaze showed her greed as she peered at his white gaping shirt and caught a glimpse of a nipple and warmly tanned skin. The hunger began to creep slowly and insidiously.

He gave the barest flicker of a smile, the sensitive woman's mouth with its delicately pronounced cupid's bow, lifting. And then he got to his feet and guided a woman, an exceedingly attractive blonde woman onto the floor. Sophie was drawn into the dance; it was mentally and physically challenging, each movement expertly executed. She leant forward, her mouth opening in a crescent of pleasure as the electrical thrills shot through her.

After a while he unbuttoned his tuxedo and, shrugging it off, threw it over a chair and it was then Sophie noticed the spear sharp, stiletto heels and the slim wrists with the elegant woman's Chanel watch, and she felt her cheeks flare. Why, it's a woman, she realised. I've been staring at a woman who dresses like a man. I've been staring at a dyke. But how thrilling to see a woman dancing with a woman.

The dance finished and the woman having retrieved her tuxedo, began to walk past Sophie's table, but stopped and, cheekily drawing out a chair, sat down.

'You don't mind, do you?' she said, almost as an afterthought.

Sophie was feverish and sexually unsettled and her glance was guarded.

The woman studied her for a moment, her fingers creeping towards Sophie's and brushing hers. She had long bright red nails to match her vivid lipstick. Her stare was that of a Cleopatra, dark and mysterious and over-emphasised by the kohl.

'You were staring at me and I was enjoying it. Couldn't you see that tango was for you? Will you dance with me? All the time I danced with her, I wished it was you.' She leant across

3

the table and Sophie smelt her odour. An exotic blend of musky male cologne and the subliminal essence of sex, rising like a vapour from her humid body.

Lifting Sophie's hand she drew circles on her palm, before pressing it to her lips and drawing spirals with her tongue.

Sophie ignited in rapid little pulses of orgasm, her recalcitrant nipples firming into tight nubs and surging forward in visible rigidity, much to the woman's evident pleasure, which was bestowed with a direct appreciation and moistening of her lips. Sophie regretted her choice of dress; she'd known it was unsuitable for a hot summer night in a club and it was now clinging to her curvy body as she perspired.

'I'm Ludmilla,' the woman said and the scrape of a nail on her palm opened a door to Sophie's sex and she felt a gripping and breathless surge of passion as she studied Ludmilla's fierce tango beauty.

'I'm Sophie.'

'Then come along Sophie, let's dance.'

'I can't dance very well. I'm too large in the hips to look elegant.'

'Nonsense! Larger women can dance very well.' Nudging her chair closer, Ludmilla slipped her arm around Sophie's waist, easing her to her feet. 'It feels like a good body to me. A luscious, *sex* body.' She emphasised the word sex with a curious sibilant hiss.

'I can't dance,' Sophie objected. 'I have no sense of rhythm.'

Ludmilla laughed. 'If you can make sex, you can dance. Sex is dance.'

But I don't do that well either, Sophie reflected. Self-analysis terrified her. It made her knock on the closed doors of her sexual consciousness. She sensed herself stiffen.

'Loosen up.' Ludmilla was holding her perilously close, her pelvis grinding into Sophie's. 'You have to be looser, darling.'

She drew Sophie into her arms and pressed her mouth close to her ear. Sophie thought she felt the tip of a wet tongue caress in yet another spiral. When Ludmilla drew back she was embracing Sophie's face with lingering invisible kisses. One at

4

the corner of her mouth, one at her lips. In response Sophie's mouth opened in erotic invitation.

'I teach dance and I know inner passion when I see it. It's all about freedom of expression. Dance is the best form of sexual therapy and I'm never wrong.' Her fingers skimmed Sophie's cheek. 'I can tell when a woman needs some therapy. Now, I'll give you the first lesson in sex dance.'

With Ludmilla's hand pressed into the small of her back, Sophie was squeezed against the warm mound of Ludmilla's sex and as Ludmilla's legs forced apart her own, so then Sophie's sex warmth was further compressed to Ludmilla's.

They began to move and the gentle rubbing friction struck a match of excitement in Sophie and the plug of ice began to warm. Sophie rested her hands on the warm tango body and pressed her mouth to Ludmilla's soft cheek. Ludmilla's lips, in turn, found her ear, the tip of her tongue circling the erogenous auricle like a bee around a honey pot.

'You want a woman to love you. Your voice says one thing and your body another.'

Ludmilla's hands slithered down to Sophie's buttocks and she rotated her hand across the fleshy pillows before stroking Sophie's nipples with the back of her hand in the merest suggestion of seduction. Sophie shuddered. She could feel the warm pulsing sex seed gestating in her belly. Ludmilla's sex heat was now melting the freezing ice between her legs.

They sat back down at the table and Ludmilla pulled her chair closer so they were now sitting with their thighs pressed tightly together. Her stare dropped to Sophie's cleavage and there was hunger in her dark eyes.

'You didn't tread on my foot once. You have the eyes of a kitten and you walk carefully like a kitten. Did anyone ever tell you that? Mmm,' Ludmilla said. 'I thought so. Poor kitten.' Her gaze hovered over Sophie's lips which were swollen as if a lover had nibbled them.

Sophie didn't think she had pretty lips, but Ludmilla passed her finger over them.

'Come to my studio tomorrow at two o'clock. It's number 11, Rue Montaigne. I have the old apartment above the clinic.

If you get lost just ask for Ludmilla. Everyone knows me there. I was once the most famous dancer in Buenos Aires.'

'I don't think so.' Sophie smiled. 'For one thing, I couldn't afford your fees.'

'Lame excuses, always lame excuses.' Her eyes flashed in her arresting face. 'But it's free, darling, because we're already friends, aren't we?' Then after a beat. 'Well, aren't we?'

'Yes,' Sophie said cautiously. 'Yes, I think so.'

'Good, since I want us to be friends, very special friends. I want to do this and I don't expect sexual favours in return. I'm simply being a philanthropist in the manner of sex and I intend to help you find your rhythm.'

Sophie had become a burning candle. The match had touched her wick and she was beginning to burn so brightly the drops of meltwater were dripping down her thighs.

An open side door, out of which seeped the tantalising strains of salsa, led up a staircase into a corridor with the studio overlooking the boulevard at the end.

When Sophie arrived Ludmilla poked her head around the door and grinned at her. Her hair was fastened back in butterfly clips and her lips were painted in the same violent red, sex lipstick. She wore a revealing leotard scooped away at the thighs and which rode so high up her crotch, Sophie could see a fringe of dark pubic curls. She was staring so hard her cheeks were burning.

'I found you something to wear. You don't have a leotard? I didn't think so.' She led Sophie into the dance studio, which had a wooden floor and mirrors and bars along the wall.

'Change into this, darling.' She held up a black lycra leotard, the kind Sophie would never have chosen because she knew it would be tight and over-exaggerate the signposts to her sex, she'd rather conceal. Nonetheless, she took it.

Sophie went into the small cubicle at the end of the room. It was little more than a box with a half door and an old curtain hanging on broken hooks. Ludmilla watched her in the reflection of a mirror. It was the look of a sexual voyeur, but for once it didn't seem to matter. Sophie was full of a new and

6

simmering sense of dangerous sexuality as if Ludmilla's embraces last night had made her bolder. She wanted her buttons pressed; she needed to push the boundaries of her sexuality, just to prove something to herself.

It wasn't as if she tried to be deliberately provocative, but the sounds of the tango, issuing forth from an old tape recorder on a table in the corner, made her so. Sophie undressed slowly like a stripper. She bent over, exhibiting her generous breasts with her rose pink nipples, allowing the breasts to fall forward, before she placed first one foot and then the other into the leotard which, as she'd thought, was far too tight, and required her to shimmy her hips and jiggle her breasts.

When she stepped outside, Ludmilla's glance seduced her. Placing her hands on Sophie's hips she turned her around, her hands and fingers dancing.

Ludmilla was as tall and slender as a pole and her exceedingly high stilettos further accentuated her splendid legs, which were strong and flexible and astonishingly sexy. Sophie quivered, aware of a wet ripple throughout her sex. Thank goodness it was a black leotard since her sex juice would not show. For this reason she felt able to indulge the clutching spasms of her sex muscles, the wildly exciting contraction and relaxation, and therefore force the melting of the ice plug a little more.

'You're so stiff.' Ludmilla's fingers sensuously dug into Sophie's shoulder muscles then down the length of her spine. 'Stand up like this. Stretch and flex like a cat.' Ludmilla bent over, and flexed her arms, drawing in her belly as she bowed her spine and stuck out her pert little breasts. 'Now, lean on the bar, that's it, buttocks out. I'll show you some exercises so you can loosen up.'

'I can do that,' Sophie said triumphantly, wanting to impress. And, to prove her point, she leant forward and, extending her leg in one fluid movement, raised it high, so her buttocks tightened.

'Excellent, so you dance after all. I knew you had a secret.'

Ludmilla stroked Sophie's hips and her hands moved all over her body, and as they did so the hands made love to

Sophie. A stroke here, a squeeze there. Each place she fondled seemed to have a secret key which Ludmilla turned, causing the warm liquid river to flow even faster within Sophie. It was impossible not to stink of sex, she thought crudely. You would have to stink of sex, in this heat with this kind of stimulation and such tight clothing.

'I think we're ready. Salsa or tango?' Ludmilla asked as she drew a circle in the air with her toe.

'Tango,' Sophie said without hesitation.

'A good choice. The tango is so much passion.'

Ludmilla, supple and androgynously irresistible, glided across the floor, her body dissolving into arabesques as her hands and legs described the dance of passion and seduction, and in Ludmilla's case, the added sensuality of the dance of courtship. It was a fascinating and disturbing demonstration of the power of controlled sex.

Sophie returned each day to the studio and each day Ludmilla coaxed the sex to the surface of her skin, while she melted away the plug of ice. Ludmilla used her legs and hips and hands to teach Sophie female sex without the use of words and from the perspective of dance. It was silent seduction by tango and it had begun to warm Sophie through every cell of her being.

Then, one day, Ludmilla pressed her leg to Sophie's, and the bewitching foot with the naughty stiletto heel, trapped her calf and Sophie held her breath as the foot with incredible self-control seduced first her ankle and then her calf, before reaching all the way up her leg, where coming to rest on the sex, Ludmilla leant into Sophie and pressed her knee into Sophie's crotch, studying her lips and flicking out her tongue to taste Sophie's mouth as she did so.

On that day Sophie lost her tenseness completely and the ice inside her became molten liquid coming to the boil. She felt she could stretch her body and sex in new ways. She was no longer tight, but loose and flowing all the way through her body.

Ludmilla smiled secretly as her finger traced Sophie's rigid nipples through the leotard. She seemed very serious.

'Take it off now,' she said. 'Take your leotard off slowly. Do a sexy dance for me, I promise I won't eat you. Look.' Much to Sophie's amazement she bent over again and peered up at Sophie from between her parted legs; before standing back up, she sensuously began to wriggle out of her own leotard.

It was compelling and erotic to watch the lean man-like body with its pert breasts emerging like a python shedding its skin. First one breast appeared, tawny hued, enhanced by the nub of her dark nipple which was as hard as a raisin, and then the other. Next, a neat sashay of the hips and Ludmilla peeled the leotard down over her firm belly and dancer's hips. All the time dancing, as she exhibited her muscular buttocks and long dancer's legs. Finally, she was completely naked except for the stilettos, and turning around she placed her hands on her hips.

Sophie gasped. Ludmilla was so beautiful. Her pubis was flat, unlike Sophie's, and sprinkled with short black curly hair – the wet slit juicily tempting.

She came to Sophie and wriggled Sophie's leotard down over her breasts before, legs akimbo, she held herself rigid, her muscular legs quivering and with remarkable self-control, she leant forward and cradled Sophie's plenteous breasts in her hand, tenderly kissing each nipple before ferociously ripping Sophie's leotard right down and kicking it away with her toe.

Ludmilla's eyes smouldered and her carmine lips parted in invitation as she gazed at Sophie's sex with its brush of thick dark hair so completely opposite in appearance to her own.

She held out her arms and they danced, except this time, Ludmilla's hands searched between her legs and Sophie, unable to sustain the rhythm of the dance, kept faltering.

Ludmilla gripped her wrist and together they ran, giggling, through the studio and up a staircase and into Ludmilla's tiny bedroom high up at the top of the apartment where the curtains were drawn and only a tiny slither of light showed.

Ludmilla tumbled onto the bed as, down below, the strains of tango that would provide the perfect accompaniment to their tangoing bodies, echoed throughout the building.

Ludmilla's strong legs tangled with Sophie's, pinning her to the bed and then she sat up, smoothing her hands down her fabulous body.

Sophie peered at her legs with the tiny sex nestled at the top. It was an extraordinary sex, she speculated. Boyish, flat and barely there and yet strikingly erotic in its seeping ripeness, and with enough of a hint of the masculine to start a raging fire in Sophie.

Ludmilla held herself very still in a totally self-controlled state of passion. But Sophie could feel the energy thrumming beneath the skin.

'Tango makes me so passionate.' Ludmilla sighed, as her finger squeezed Sophie's sex and slithered up and down the wet slit. 'The tango opens me up and now it opens you.' Throwing back her head she laughed. 'Now, you know why Argentineans are so passionate. It's because the music of the tango is always flowing through our veins, and it makes us into sex.'

She cupped Sophie's chin, fondling her mouth with her lips; the tip of her tongue caressing while her hands moved over Sophie's body, starting small fires here and there.

'Oh.' Sophie gasped as Ludmilla seized her clit between her finger and thumb and tugged on it gently.

'You dance with passion now.'

'Yes.' Sophie smiled. 'But only with you.'

'Good, good.' Ludmilla purred as she placed her knees on either side of Sophie's hips and began lowering herself slowly up and down to the accompaniment of the sultry sounds of the tango. Each time she came down, she ground her boyish, barely-there sex into Sophie's, and soon Sophie began to rise to meet her and her hands came onto Ludmilla's hips.

Ludmilla took Sophie's hand and she pressed three fingers together before making her push the fingers into her cunt.

Sophie teased and fingered the tight little purse lips, while Ludmilla cried and stretched her lean limbs up and out of her passion, her arms forming shapes in the air and her dancer's muscles clenching and releasing Sophie's inquisitive fingers.

Ludmilla threw back her head and, cupping her breasts, she stretched like a panther and gave a guttural shriek of delight.

Sophie massaged the tender inner sex muscles with her fingers and the muscles released her and gripped, and released again, as Ludmilla kissed her and engaged her in a teasing game of jousting tongues.

'I have a surprise for you,' she said, clambering off the bed. Strolling over to an old French wardrobe on her high heels, she opened the doors and took something out. 'It's my surprise for Sophie.'

Ludmilla fastened some complicated straps around her slim hips and then she turned around.

Sophie gasped.

The strap-on had a large and exquisitely upturned penis which thrust invitingly at Sophie, as Ludmilla balancing expertly on the heels, strutted towards her with her hips thrust out and gyrating.

Sophie stood up and Ludmilla moved into her arms. They held each other gently at first and Sophie clutched the muscular buttocks so the greedy penis nuzzled her sex.

I'm dancing the tango, Sophie thought as the cock slipped between her moist fleshy lips. I always dreamt of sex with the tango.

'I think I know your fantasy, and now I'll unlock you.' Ludmilla smiled. 'Now we dance tango and we have sex tango.'

The penis teased. It entered and retreated and, with each savage thrust of the tango, it penetrated deeper, finding no ice but only molten lava.

Ludmilla span her like a top and, lifting Sophie up with her strong dancer's arms, lowered her onto the cock, while Sophie, her thighs now powerful from dance, gripped them around Ludmilla's waist.

The music continued to play and the passionate thrust of the tango became the passionate embrace of love.

A Dip in the Pool
by Eve Diamond

I checked my boobs were tucked in properly before leaving the changing room. How many times now had I tried swimming lessons? Maybe this beginners' course for nervous adults would help me show my husband I wasn't a total failure.

The pool was a seductive turquoise as I approached the women waiting at the shallow end. A slim blonde in a navy blue vest and tracky bottoms stood, clipboard in hand, ticking off names. She looked up and locked gazes with me.

Her hair was the colour of ripe corn. She wore it scooped into a scrunchie but there was no disguising its shine. Her skin was a healthy honey tone even under the strip lighting. Beside her, I felt pasty, lumpy and inadequate, until she smiled as if genuinely pleased to see me.

'Hi, I'm Megan Besant, your instructor. Hopefully you must be either, um, Ms Jelly or Ms Clarkson?'

I shouldn't have laughed at someone else's surname but I did. We both did. Suddenly it seemed the sun had come out. 'I'm Julie Clarkson,' I said. 'But maybe Julie Jelly would be more appropriate this evening.'

Her eyes danced. 'You'll be fine, Julie. You're going to lose all that fearfulness. You'll see. And please call me Megan – or Meg if it's easier. You're happy with first names, I hope?'

'Yes, please.' I liked the way she checked with me. And her warmth was a real stress buster because I'd stopped trembling. I recognise now, it was at that moment I began lusting after Megan Besant.

Driving home later, the whiff of pool water clung to my

skin. My hair was a mess of barbed wire so I let myself in and went straight upstairs. Greg would still be on the golf course. These long daylight hours were a godsend to a workaholic. He was at his desk by six in the morning and often not home till ten.

'Wait till we go on holiday, Jules,' he'd said the night before. 'You'll have my total attention then.' He'd kissed me and turned over. Soon he was snoring. I'd been uptight about my swimming lesson and desperate to bring myself to orgasm. I risked waking up Greg as my fingers searched out my special places. But I couldn't just lie there sleepless and longing.

Now I stood under the shower, lathering my skin. As the rich magnolia perfume banished the chlorine, all I could think of was being fucked. Greg was OK in bed, not sensational but OK. I was still trying to get him to loosen up a little, but since he got bitten by the golf bug, sex between us hadn't always been too great. I was barely dry when I padded back into the master bedroom, wrapped in a fluffy bath sheet. I put on a Kirsty MacColl CD, let the towel fall and stretched out on the jade satin counterpane.

It was strange. Instead of my favourite movie stud appearing to spice up my fantasy, a slim woman with golden hair drifted into my consciousness. She sat on the bed, eyes travelling over my naked body. I watched her devour each and every curve. At last she met my gaze with a question in her eyes.

'Yes,' I said, letting both my hands roam over my breasts.

Her dirty chuckle sent waves of lust rippling from my nipples to my cunt. She stood up and peeled off her vest and trousers. Underneath, she wore a black sports bra and a pair of black silk boxers. The severe underwear clung to her honed body. There was nothing unfeminine about her but she was the exact opposite of me with my billowing boobs and marshmallow thighs.

She moved, kneeling in front of me, parting my legs. 'Relax,' she said. 'I'm here to help you. Forget everything else in the world and just go with the flow.'

I could feel those fantasy fingers. I dragged my own fingers

14

away from my screaming nipples and touched the soft skin at the top of my legs. It was my own fingers that parted my pussy lips and discovered how wet I was. But my oh-so familiar touch wasn't right. I sat up and grabbed the vibrator from my bedside cabinet. The whirring lulled me as I settled back and closed my eyes, letting the lip of the phallic pretender lap my folds and frills.

I did sound effects too. I made her ... yes, OK, I made Megan talk to me, whispering words I knew could only come from another woman.

'I know what you want, Julie. You want to feel yourself lifting, drifting until you're floating. All you care about is riding the waves. Ride with me, darling. I'm using a little lube on your bumhole, Julie. Don't be nervous. All I care about is making you come. I want to watch you come for me – watch you creaming and screaming. See you topple over the edge of that big, big wave we're building.'

Her voice was liquid butterscotch in my head. I was hypnotising myself with my own erotic yearning. I imagined that saucy finger insinuating itself into my bottom. It was a terrific turn-on. I clenched my bum cheeks and felt the first of the chain of tremors signposting my climax. I imagined Megan's finger pushing deeper. 'Naughty finger,' I scolded, 'going where it shouldn't.' Again there was that knowing chuckle rippling inside my head.

My breathing was raucous as "she" played the vibrator like I knew she would. Slow and deliberate. Painting it around my slippery softness; edging its tip inside and inching it along the love tunnel. Another spasm and now I was panting, hovering somewhere in cyber sex-land.

'Little tigress. I love watching you getting turned on. Come on, sweetie. Talk dirty to me. Say anything you want,' her voice crooned. Nobody had ever before given me such an erotic invitation.

I was panting. The sound of my own arousal stimulated me as much as my own hand controlling the vibrator. But I still pretended it was Megan doing it. My legs were bent and parted, making me vulnerable although I knew I was in safe hands. At some point – can't remember when – I'd dragged a pillow under my thighs so I could insert a finger inside my anus. I was so wet that I wasn't sure which was lube and which was my own juices.

I spoke out loud. 'I have to come. You're going to make me. Then you must lie down with me. Put your arms round me. Push your breasts against me. Then I want you to suck my nipples. I want to feel you sucking on them, deep inside me. Inside my hot wet cunt. Then I want you to lick me down there. Suck my juices. I'll watch you. Doing it. Please ... oh please, Meg.'

I pictured that corn-gold hair tumbling loose over her cheeks as she worked my clitoris, taking me to screaming point. Then she completed the sweet torture by fastening her lips round my engorged tip and sucking me till I came, thrashing and writhing under her like a snarling Mrs Rochester desperate to set fire to her husband.

But it was Megan setting fire to me as I roared towards the crest of that big wave we'd created. The tension relaxed as I was consumed by a big, bountiful orgasm.

Greg wined and dined me at the weekend. When we got home afterwards he opened more wine. I'd already drunk quite a bit so I went upstairs and put on the provocative outfit he loves me to wear. I never regard myself as a sex object because when I dress in fuck-me lingerie, he's at my mercy. He'll even behave a little out of character, if I get lucky.

I stood before the mirror and watched myself squeezing into the lacy two-piece. The balcony bra offered twin globes, creamy flesh spilling over burgundy lace ruffles. My nipples were almost escaping the fabric, but not quite. The high-cut knickers held a secret. There was a split crotch with jealous silver ribbons guarding the gateway but just waiting to be undone.

I walked downstairs. He'd opened the patio doors and the dusky July evening, ripe with musk rose and lavender, drifted into the room.

When he turned towards me, his eyes darkened. 'I have to fuck you.' He put down his glass.

I moved towards the open door. 'Let's make love outside.'

He was looking flustered. I knew he had a hard-on. I knew he'd been looking forward to his Friday night fuck, but didn't I deserve a little consideration? A little sweet-talking after a week of solitary evenings. I didn't intend telling him about my swimming lessons.

'Come on,' I coaxed. I reached for the crimson throw draped across the cream couch. 'Nobody's going to know. It'll be romantic.' I didn't add, "For a change".

No way was our garden overlooked. Greg had come from ambitious council house boy to savvy businessman with not inconsiderable help from *moi*. We lived in a sought-after village. Our four-bedroom detached house was encircled by a high wall. The nearby properties, screened by tall trees, were built at angles determined by some unknown architect. I can sunbathe naked if I wish.

'Jules, I want you naked on the bed so I can fuck your brains out.'

The wine had loosened his tongue. And given me courage. 'I thought you liked finger-fucking me when I'm wearing these knickers. What's your hurry?'

He groaned. I walked slowly past him, still clutching the throw. I paused on the patio but opted for the lawn, swinging my arse as I went down the wide steps leading to the garden. He wanted to get his rocks off without the foreplay he knows I adore. And need. I recognised his need but the devil was in me.

He was beside me in an instant. 'You win,' he said.

'G'boy,' I said. I spread the throw over the grass and lay down, parting my legs and letting those silver ribbons beg to be untied.

He did his best to make me come. After alcohol he's less inhibited, but he doesn't like to hang around and even the crotchless knickers didn't hold his attention for long. He's tone-deaf when it comes to cunt harmony and I knew I should persevere and teach him. But that night my mind was awash with sensuous images of Megan.

I tried to keep pace as Greg pumped away, filling me but not fulfilling me. Suddenly I began whispering soft filthy words, half to myself, half to the evening air. I knew from the grunts that he was close to coming so I licked my thumb and slipped it down to rub myself. His rhythm slowed a tad. I only needed a little help and, as he sped up again, jabbing and grinding, I was there.

When I called out, it was her name I shouted. 'I'm coming, Meg ...'

He took me in his arms, obviously delighted with the way I was smiling. And it occurred to me that if he'd heard me while he was lost in his own orgasm, he'd have assumed I was calling his name.

Next swimming session I tried to relax as Megan told us what to do. To my disappointment, she was avoiding eye contact with me. But I persevered with the tasks, practising moving my legs the right way but with the comfort blanket of floats. She didn't single me out at all and, when a male colleague turned up as we quit the pool, I felt an idiotic pang of jealousy.

The following week Greg was away on business. The first day I made coffee for the cleaning lady and wandered round the garden, dead-heading roses. I was supposed to do stuff towards the looming village fête but felt too restless to settle to it.

Greg always said I was a man's woman – sweet, vulnerable, lovely to come home to. I'd given up my job when we got married. I was a receptionist in the hotel where he'd booked accommodation one night. After I checked him in, he'd asked what time I came off duty.

Greg had waited till 10 p.m. when my shift ended. He took me down the road to a country house hotel where he'd previously stayed but which was chock-a-block that night. We had drinks and coffee and then he drove me back to my flat. We exchanged contact details and agreed to meet for lunch the next day.

He was a widower. He invited me to spend the next weekend with him. I swapped shifts because I thought he was sexy with his cropped grey hair and panther-like stride. I gawped in amazement when he drove up to this fabulous pad and I fell into his hands like a ripe plum dropping off the tree. I was bored with my job and starved of sex since my last relationship ended. We couldn't get enough of each other and were married two months later. My life was transformed.

But after the initial floaty pink cloud stage, I began to feel undervalued. I had one or two jobs then tried playing Domestic Goddess. Boring. Now, with another evening on my own, I was at my computer, discovering websites. A whole new world unfolded.

The women on the sites I visited were mega beautiful. I clicked on image after image, seeing tongues tasting, lips kissing, fingers feeling. Blondes licked redheads and brunettes nuzzled women with rich brown hair, shaven heads even. I hit on a video clip of two naked girls kissing on a bed. One was blonde like Megan, one raven-haired like me. I was so turned on that I whimpered. My hand crept up my thigh and I pushed two fingers inside my panties so I could watch their bodies, slippery with baby oil and writhing, while I frigged myself to a climax.

Megan was in my head, in my fingers, in my bed. I wondered what she'd taste like. Whether she called out when she came. I wondered if she'd be horrified to know that a bored housewife lusted after her.

At the start of Session Three, Megan asked us all to sit on the edge of the pool and dangle our feet. She stripped off her tracksuit, revealing a shapely body in a sleek red racer back. I shivered with excitement as she jumped into the water and stood in front of our row of eight. I sat next to Ms Jelly who was a pleasant woman, a tad phobic about the water, but who'd confided at the first session she was desperate to learn before her children realised how petrified she was.

Megan asked each of us exactly what motivated us to learn. She wondered how we felt we were progressing.

When my turn came, I said, 'My husband's taking me to the Maldives in September. I've never learnt to swim. Greg's promised to teach me on holiday and I'd like to surprise him.'

I sounded, even to me, the perfect, pampered wife. And I felt trivial and convinced that Megan would write me off as vacuous and well-suited to having too much time on my hands. I didn't want her to think of me like that.

'You need to do this for yourself, Julie,' she said. And then she reached under the water and squeezed each of my ankles. The gentle pressure of her fingers echoed up both thighs and discharged a thunderbolt between them.

When Ms Jelly disclosed her reason, Megan folded her arms. I watched the cleft between her breasts deepen and swallowed. Hard.

'Not one of you is incapable of swimming,' she said. 'You can do it, all of you. The question is, ladies, will you? You've practised the strokes. Now, into the water please …'

As she instructed, I leaned forward; arms stretched in front of me, trying to convince myself I could lie on the surface and lunge towards the side. Three or four of the others achieved this. Jelly and I froze.

'Stop thinking too much,' a voice whispered. 'Remember. Go with the flow.'

I never wear a bathing cap and Megan's breath was warm in my ear. My nipples stiffened. I wanted her hands on me so much I had to close my eyes and take a deep breath. Next thing I was clutching the pool edge, leaving poor Jelly on her own.

I stood up and looked at Megan. 'Well done,' she mouthed.

I felt a hot rush of pleasure as I waded back to the point from where we were gliding. Once more I gave myself to the water and arrived poolside.

My fellow-learner staggered forward. 'It's no good,' she wailed. 'I'm useless.'

Megan held her elbow. 'Julie, just stay where you are, would you?'

She spoke firmly to Ms Jelly. 'Pretend Julie's your little girl. She's three metres away and she's drowning. Nobody else is around. What do you do?'

I watched in amazement as Jelly plunged forward, arms and legs whacking in a wild doggy paddle. But she made it. She grabbed me the instant she was within reach and my swimsuit sagged, exposing my bare breasts. Ms Jelly was so joyful that she didn't even notice. She was too busy calling out to the others.

I knew Megan was watching me hitch up my swimsuit. I felt my nipples graze the wet fabric. The urge to touch them was overwhelming. The beat between my thighs was unbearable. I almost sobbed as my throat dried, even though I'd swallowed gallons of pool water.

'And you, Julie. Well done too. Walk back to me now and do it again.'

I waded towards her, forcing myself to drag my eyes away from her pert breasts, outlined by clinging lycra. A tiny smile played around her lips. At that moment I'd have done anything she asked. And I think she knew it.

After the session, everyone hurried to get off home, as usual. They were probably relieved another hour's torment was over. Adult learners have a hard time overcoming hang-ups and bad memories. I was having a hard time in my cubicle. I'd showered but I'd forgotten my shampoo and couldn't be bothered to use the dispenser. I wound a small towel around my head and started to pull my panties over my still-damp thighs.

Then I heard the connecting door to the foyer open and shut.

'Am I the last one?' I called, anticipating silence.

'Julie?' I recognised Megan's urgent, husky voice.

My heart raced as I wrenched the curtain open and stood there, towel hugged to my breasts. Two steps and she tugged the curtain across and loosened her robe. My eyes dropped to those delectable round dumplings, nipples taut and firm as cherries. The triangle of pubic hair halfway down her body gleamed wet gold like the hair plastered to her head.

'I tried to keep away,' she said. 'I know you're not …'

'Just stay,' I whispered.

I was drowning. Her skin was cool; her lips firm, her tongue precocious, flicking over mine to tiptoe inside my mouth. We were the same height and, when her breasts pressed against mine, electricity pierced me. My nipples reacted and she stopped what she was doing and began tasting them. I arched my neck, wondering what I was supposed to do.

She sensed it. 'You've made huge strides tonight. Just go

with the flow.'

It was déjà vu. I pulled her up so we faced each other then cupped her breasts in my hands, thumbing the nipples, coaxing them.

She groaned. 'Fuck, that's so lovely. But I wanted to make you come first.'

'No. You first,' I said. I knelt on my soggy towel and began tonguing her centre. Totally new territory. I couldn't believe I was exploring another woman's secret places. I knew what the anatomy was but I didn't know Meg's sexual wiring. And I didn't want to flounder – in the pool or out.

I released her. 'What do you like?' My voice sounded more confident than I felt.

'I like what you're doing.' She was breathless. How lovely.

I had to make sure. 'Will anyone come in?'

'I locked the main door after the others.'

I can't describe my excitement at hearing she'd made a conscious decision. But still I kept the curtains closed. And in our private domain I travelled further along the erotic scale than I'd ever travelled with any man. All I had to do was do what I enjoyed having done to me.

Her squeals and moans accompanied the sound of my tongue lapping and my lips sucking her clit into a tiny erect penis. I brought her to the edge of ecstasy then felt her cream against my mouth as she shuddered in my arms. She sank down on the floor and we cuddled each other, letting the peace envelop us like a velvet cloak. I was waiting for more. And she knew it. She was as expert at this kind of loving as she was in the pool.

'I don't want this to end but there are things I must do. Are you free tonight? So we can go somewhere more comfortable.'

I caught my breath. 'You can follow me back to my place if you like.'

'Really? No jealous husband likely to rush out with drawn sword?'

I giggled. Blushed like a schoolgirl. 'Nope. He's away this week.'

'And I'm here to lead you astray. Meet you in the foyer in

ten minutes then.'

I got dressed knowing I'd opened Pandora's Box and couldn't wait to explore the contents.

Driving home in my ridiculously expensive car, with Megan following in her old Renault, I was trembling at my own audacity. I was bringing a lover onto my territory, the home I shared with my husband. But I didn't intend his shadow to come between Megan and me, so to speak. I was aching for her, not him.

She made no comment about the luxury. We were both dressed casually. Our hair like a week of wet Sundays. I locked and bolted the front door before offering her a drink.

She stood there in her practical tracksuit. I wore leggings and a lightweight fleece.

'You're going all polite on me,' she said. 'A glass of wine will relax you. Can we take it to bed? I want to explore you.'

Not only was I introducing a lover into this home of married coupledom but I was taking her into my bed. She followed me into the kitchen as I went to the fridge, trembling fingers fumbling for the bottle.

'Is white OK?'

She shrugged. 'Whatever you like.'

'Are you hungry?'

She just smiled. I found glasses and she unscrewed the cap and poured the wine. She dipped a finger into hers and moved closer so she could paint my lips with chardonnay. I was already dizzy with wanting. I wanted her to take me on a journey and she must have seen the longing in my eyes because she collected her glass and walked into the hallway.

I pulled myself together and preceded her upstairs, hesitating at the door of the first guest bedroom before continuing down the corridor to the master. I went over to the king-size bed and parked my glass. She too placed her wine on her bedside cabinet and kicked off her trainers.

'Oh Julie,' she said. 'Would you prefer it if I had a massive prick?'

I didn't reply. Just pulled my top over my head and reached round to unfasten my bra letting my breasts spill out for her.

She sat down. Kept staring. I wriggled out of my leggings and stood there in my pale pink hip huggers. I pushed them down and stepped out of them when they pooled around my ankles.

I sat on the bed and sipped my wine. We'd smell the pool water on each other. Until the scent of our juices drove the chlorine away. I wanted what began in the shallows to deepen. There's nothing quite as seductive as foreplay when it's performed well. And foreplay comes in many forms.

She drank some wine before removing her clothing. She made no attempt to be provocative but the way she held my gaze accelerated the pulse between my legs. I clenched both fists to stop me from playing with myself.

'There's no law against touching yourself,' she murmured. Then she was beside me on the bed. 'Go on, Julie. I'll drink some more of this fabulous wine while I watch you frolic.'

I'd never masturbated in front of anyone else before. I unclenched my fists and drank more wine too. Then I lay back and stretched. My hands found my nipples but the pounding below demanded attention. Slowly I brushed my fingers across the damp tangle between my legs. Tousled wet hair on our heads and our pussies – the thought was a turn-on. The evening was a domino run of turn-ons. And it wasn't over yet.

Megan put down her glass. 'You're so beautiful,' she whispered. She pushed her face against my cunt, nuzzling her nose and mouth into me. I pushed one finger into my mouth and sucked on it, groaning as I pushed in and out. I longed for cock. Was I going to enjoy girly play?

What happened next was a revelation.

'I've got something for you,' she said, pulling away to reach under the bed. I hadn't noticed, but she must have brought her bag upstairs because she produced a tube and a brush.

'Chocolate body paint,' she said. 'I'm going to paint your nipples then suck them. You get to do the same for me afterwards if you like.'

Afterwards? After what? After she'd played me like a tautly strung instrument and brought me to the end of my rope before she let me come. My whole body tingled. My mind, my heart, my stomach and my cunt were in thrall to this woman. I didn't care about anything now. Just lay there while she did what she wanted. I'd known her for such a brief time and I was permitting intimacies it had taken me weeks to grant to any man.

I stretched my arms above my head, offering a bare canvas.

'You're beautiful,' she said again. And I felt the first flick of sable resonate through my body.

I smelt the chocolate, sweet vanilla scenting bitter cocoa. I felt the stickiness as she painted layer after layer on my nipples. I looked down at two glossy, greasy, dark discs like the stage bling of an exotic dancer. I wondered what the chocolate would taste like when my turn came to feast. Then I stopped wondering as Megan began tonguing. She crooned as she set about her task. Slowly and deliberately. Eventually she chuckled and raised her head, displaying the smeary mouth of a two-year-old let loose in the sweetie tin.

'Don't stop,' I called. I was on the brink of orgasm. She fell upon me again and there was no going back. For the first time in my life I was climaxing simply by someone sucking my breasts.

But my jealous cunt wouldn't be ignored. I began to writhe and whimper as soon as the first delicious ripples ceased. I craved more powerful sensations. Megan again tuned in to my needs.

She turned away to take another dip into her magician's bag. This time she held a dildo. I caught my breath.

'Down to me to control,' she said. 'Like a man controls how he drives into you, I'll decide how fast or ... how slow I slide this guy in and out. It's formidable, don't you think? I'll go easy ... at first.'

It was certainly bigger than any flesh-and-blood one I'd experienced. Megan reached for the lube and I felt the cool gel slathering my pussy lips. No way did I want to close my eyes and miss seeing her play me with her awesome Technicolor dream cock.

'Such a pretty little slit,' she murmured. 'How amazing it can take this huge, thrusting dick.' She was pushing the dildo slowly inside me. First my fleshy lips, then my walls, accepted the big stranger eagerly.

'She likes it,' she sang. 'Julie likes my huge cock fucking her.'

She increased the tempo.

'Please,' I gasped. 'More. More and faster. Please. Yes.'

'Greedy girl. Greedy cock-hungry girl. Shall she get what she wants?'

'Yes. Do it. Do it.' I was begging.

Megan rocked back and fore, sucking air through her lovely mouth as she fucked. I was taking almost all the dildo. With her other hand she was rubbing my clit. I was helpless and loving it.

'Beautiful, beautiful fuck,' I yelled. 'Make me come. I have to come.'

So I've kept on coming. And learning. Greg knows that swimming nights I go for a curry with a friendly, single mum called Sharon Jelly. I leave a gourmet supper in the fridge for him. After each session, I follow Megan back to her flat where she continues her instruction helped by a shedload of sex toys.

We tease and we titillate, we suck and we strum. She's bought me panties to stimulate my clit when I walk. I buy her violet creams she lets melt in her mouth while she's eating me. We read one another's body like we read our own.

At the end of the learners' course I enrolled as an improver. By September I was swimming confident widths.

'Are you ready to jump in the deep end?' Greg teased me as I packed the day before our holiday.

'No problem,' I said.

I've decided to pretend fear in the water so Greg will encourage me to go on the residential course Meg's planning to run. The venue is a fabulous country house hotel, though fortunately not the one where he sometimes stays. Now I've taken the plunge, I need to keep going with the flow.

And, slowly, I'm teaching Greg a few girly tricks.

Hot Pursuit
by Lynn Lake

Constable Eva Lemieux was parked behind a Connors Strawberry Farms billboard out on Highway 12, allegedly monitoring the radar gun mounted up on her dashboard, checking for speeders. But it was mid-afternoon of a warm, sunny, drowsy day, and Eva had just polished off a large lunch complete with homemade cheesecake at a restaurant in Argyle, and the highway was sparsely populated with vehicular traffic; and so Eva was dozing behind the wheel of her RCMP cruiser, in the soft velvet shade of the billboard.

The petite, dark-haired, dark-eyed French Canadian had only been on the Force three months, and rural southern Manitoba was her first posting. It was proving anything but exciting. The area was Bible-belt country, law abiders outnumbering lawbreakers by about 5,000 to 1.

She settled down lower in the comfortable bucket seat of the cruiser and contentedly smacked her lips, her hands folded across her chest, cap pulled down low. A cop had to be resourceful, replenish their resources any chance they got, anywhere they could. The young officer had to make dinner for the rest of the staff back at the stationhouse that night, after all. Something about her initiation, she dreamily recalled.

A mini-van droned by on the highway, religiously holding under the speed limit. Crickets chirped in the vast, sun-drenched field of sunflowers directly behind the cruiser, in the equally huge field of corn across the road. Somewhere far off a crow cawed and a gopher sneezed, the light summer breeze rustling the sea of green leaves.

Eva licked her lips, not thinking about dinner any more; thinking, instead, about her fellow officer, Constable Susan Orpetski. The tall, lean, blue-eyed blonde had graduated one class ahead of Eva from the Regina training academy, and had recently been transferred down south after a stint up north. Eva was thinking, particularly, of the previous night, when Susan had changed out of her uniform and into her civvies in the basement of the stationhouse, as Eva had watched.

The fingers of her right hand slipped out of her left hand and slid down onto the crotch of her dark-blue uniform pants, as she recalled Susan's lithe body, the woman's limbs long and smooth and sun-browned, mounded bottom bulging out her white cotton panties in back, pert breasts pushing out her white lycra bra in front. 'Mmmm,' Eva murmured, eyes closed, a glossy smile spreading over her full lips, fingers rubbing her pussy in her pants. The blonde had looked yummy enough to eat, like that lunch-hour cheesecake, only richer, more succulent, more satisfying.

She bit her lip, fingers rubbing faster, more firmly. She concentrated on that powerful bronze-blonde image of Susan in her skimpy underwear. Only now, the underwear was coming off.

Susan was looking at Eva staring at her, and unhooking her bra at the back. Her long arms came forward, her buff shoulders shrugging, the bra slipping off and away. Susan's breasts were high and firm and handful-sized, tan-lined, nipples pink and pointing, areolae a darker hue of coral.

Eva brushed her left hand over her chest, was blocked by her Kevlar vest. She rubbed with the right all the quicker, spreading her legs further apart. As Susan pirouetted around and slipped her fingers into her panties and arched her bum, and then slowly slid the undergarment over and down her ripe, taut, tan-lined butt cheeks. 'Yes!' Eva breathed, flooding with languorous feeling.

Susan stepped out of her fallen panties and turned back to face her fellow officer again, fully naked now. Her body blazed before Eva's dazzled eyes, as she walked closer, breasts shuddering, trim blonde pussy winking with moisture.

They were in each other's arms, Eva's suddenly naked body pressing against Susan's hot, nude body, nipples squishing together, breasts exquisitely flattening. Their mouths drew closer, lips and eyes shining …

'Mais, oui!' Eva cried, rubbing herself to the very edge of orgasm. 'I love you–'

Wham!

The RCMP officer was flung forward against the steering wheel, jolted out of her trance.

A siren blooped loudly and red and blue lights flashed brightly.

Eva pushed herself back and stared into the rearview mirror – into Susan's sparkling blue eyes in the car behind. Hastily shoving her cap up and clamping her legs closed, she shakily waved at her colleague, her face flushed and fingertips moist.

Susan switched off the siren and lights and got out of her cruiser, as Eva crawled out of her vehicle. The two women met at the back door of Eva's car, Susan in full dark-blue uniform with yellow stripe down the side of the pants, just like her colleague.

'Sleeping on the job, Constable Lemieux?' she cracked, hitching her hands onto her utility belt.

Eva blushed an even deeper shade of scarlet. 'Uh, no, I was just, um, resting my eyes for a moment. You see anyone speeding along the highway?'

Susan laughed. 'I don't know, did you?' She looked Eva up and down, admiring the woman's pretty, oval face and deep brown eyes, her lustrous black hair pulled back into a ponytail. 'You never know when something might happen. Police work can go from 0 to 100 in a split-second.'

'Around here? It's so–'

Susan shoved Eva back against the cruiser and smacked the woman's hat off her head, smacked her own wet, red mouth into Eva's lush mouth. She kissed Eva hard, hungrily, lips moving against Eva's lips.

Then she abruptly pulled back. 'Bet you weren't expecting that, now, were you?' She licked her lips, the sweet, tantalising taste of her colleague upon them.

'N–no!' Eva gasped, stunned by the suddenness of all she'd been hoping for. 'But I wouldn't object to more of the–'

A car roared by on the highway.

'Hold that thought!' Susan yelped, jumping over to the driver-side door of the cruiser and peering in. The radar gun registered 183 kilometres per hour. 'Duty calls, cutie!'

Eva grabbed up her hat and planted it on her head. Then she pushed Susan aside and yanked the cruiser door open and jumped inside. She punched the siren and light buttons, cranked the engine. Susan raced around to the other side of the vehicle, barely managing to pull her legs in after her bum before Eva put pedal to the metal.

The police tyres spat dirt and dust, and the vehicle fishtailed out from behind the billboard and onto the highway, Eva clutching the steering wheel, Susan the door.

'There he is – up ahead!' Susan yelled.

Rubber screamed on asphalt, Eva's booted foot pressing right down to the floor. 'I see him,' she gritted, her knuckles white on the wheel.

The specially-modified RCMP cruiser rocketed down the highway, gaining ground on the wildly speeding motorist.

'Black Ford Taurus – SLE!' Susan shouted, squinting.

'SHO,' Eva rasped, sweat beading her forehead below the hat brim, her eyes gleaming, face glowing.

They were half-a-kilometre behind the other car, and closing fast.

Suddenly, a plume of blue smoke rose up ahead, the Taurus swinging crazily around, rear tyres dancing across the asphalt. The vehicle rocked, righted itself, gained traction, shot ahead – straight at the oncoming cruiser.

Susan slammed her hands down on the dashboard, bracing herself for the moment Eva swerved out of the way and spun the police car around.

The cars barrelled down the shimmering strip of highway towards one another, neither vehicle giving way. 300 metres, 200 metres, 100 metres. The two police officers could see the face behind the wheel of the Taurus – a man's pale face, mouth wide open and yelling, scraggly brown hair blown wild by the wind rushing in through the open windows, eyes blazing even wilder.

'You'd better turn, Eva!' Susan cried over the full-throttle howl of the engine. 'This guy's out of his head – high as a kite!'

'I'm not turning,' Eva growled. 'I'm the law. He'll have to turn.'

Susan stared at her colleague, at the black doomsday machine racing inexorably towards them. They were only 50 metres apart, drawing together like magnets, rushing faster and faster towards one another.

'Oh my God!' Susan moaned.

20 metres, 10 metres.

The Taurus veered left, the driver frantically jerking the wheel over. They could see his quivering lips and streaming eyes as he raced by. The car sailed off the shoulder of the road and out into the cornfield, landing with a resounding thud and a mushroom cloud of dust.

Eva stomped both feet down onto the brake pedal and yanked the steering wheel over to the left, executing a perfect rubber-squealing, smoke-billowing spin-a-rama on the empty highway. The car shuddered straight and the officers' heads snapped back into alignment, now facing the direction they'd just come from.

Eva gunned the car, speeding to the spot where the other vehicle's tracks left the roadway. She skidded to a stop on the shoulder and leapt out of the cruiser, Susan right on her tail.

They ran through the bent and broken cornstalks to where the Taurus sat mired in the dirt and vegetation. The hell-raising joyrider was sitting bolt upright in his seat, staring straight ahead into the corn, his fingers embedded in the steering wheel – scared sober.

He was dazed, but unhurt.

Eva pulled him out of the car and slammed him up against the side of the vehicle, slapped handcuffs onto his bony wrists. She was shaking violently, adrenaline rushing through her small body in waves. She looked at Susan. 'See, I told you–'

Susan grabbed Eva's head and kissed her hard on the

mouth. Then she broke away, dragged the speeder by the handcuffs out to the highway and threw him into the backseat of the cruiser. She slammed the door, stalked back into the cornfield, shedding items of her uniform as she did so.

By the time she reached Eva who was still standing, shivering, by the side of the Ford, her cap and tunic were gone, her bulletproof vest and T-shirt discarded, utility belt dragging behind her, then dropping. She strode up to Eva, unhooking her white lycra bra at the back and shrugging it away, exposing her high, firm, tan-lined breasts and jutting pink nipples.

The two women grasped one another, their open mouths mashing together.

For some male police officers, the thrill of the chase might lead them to beating their captured quarry, or at least roughing them up, taking out their sky-high energy and frustration on the person responsible for so rudely disrupting their routine. But for these two female police officers, they vented their wound-up excitement on each other, loving, not hating.

Eva squeezed Susan's hot, bare upper body tight, moving her lips against Susan's moving lips, the pair devouring each other's mouths. Eva shot her tongue inside Susan's mouth, and Susan instantly twined it with her tongue, the slick pink appendages twisting and tumbling together, over and over.

Eva jerked her head back, down, panting all over Susan's heaving chest. And then she grasped the woman's breasts, thrilling at the feel of the hot, smooth, conical flesh, Susan thrilling at Eva's grip. Eva stuck out her tongue again and flicked a rigid nipple, the other rubbery nipple, squeezing Susan's breasts in her hands.

'Yes!' Susan groaned, tilting her head back, blonde hair streaming.

They were hidden from the highway by the tall stalks of corn, and wild with desire under the hot, beating sun. Eva sealed her lips around one of Susan's stiffened nipples and sucked on it. Bounced her head over to the woman's other breast and mouthed that throbbing tip, tugging on it.

Susan writhed with delight in Eva's hands, her nipples buzzing in the other woman's mouth. Then she pushed Eva back and tore at her colleague's uniform.

Eva was soon as bare-chested as Susan. Her breasts were large and round and tawny-skinned as the rest of her, darker nipples flared with feeling. Susan grasped the woman's rounded shoulders and pressed her breasts into Eva's.

Both women moaned at the soft, heated impact, their nipples and tits squeezing together. Their mouths met again, their tongues, their bodies on fire.

Boots, then pants and panties joined the clothing already strewn on the ground, the officers fully shedding their uniforms and inhibitions. They stood facing one another, starkly naked. Just two very needful, very attractive women now, all semblance of duty abandoned. They deserved each other after what they'd just been through.

They met in another heated embrace, Susan's hands plunging down Eva's curved back and latching onto the woman's plush, mounded butt cheeks. Eva moaned into Susan's mouth, feeling the woman ply her buttocks, their bare bodies melding together. Eva slid her own damp hands down and gripped Susan's pert buttocks, kneaded them, eliciting an equal moan of pleasure from her blonde lover.

The situation quickly escalated out of control, kissing and fondling spiking to licking and lapping of the most intimate kind. The women mounted the hood, then the roof of the Taurus. Eva stretched out on her back on the sun-baked black metal. Susan straddled Eva's head with her knees, planted her hands on Eva's thighs. Code 69, two women going down on one another.

The metal was hot, the charged-up pair even hotter. Susan stared down at Eva's downy-furred pussy. Eva stared up at Susan's strip-shaved slit. Susan's fingernails bit into Eva's thighs, Eva's into Susan's butt cheeks. Their tongues touched pussy simultaneously.

Both women shuddered, then licked.

Susan dragged her tongue through Eva's damp fur, lapping at the woman's pussy. Eva licked up and down Susan's glistening pink petals, tongue-stroking pussy from top to bottom.

They gasped, groaned, holding on tight and lapping away at one another, tasting each other's tangy juices. Perspiration dewed Susan's body, her buttocks trembling in Eva's hands, her head bobbing back and forth between the woman's legs. Eva's thighs twitched and jumped beneath Susan's hands, her dizzy head moving rapidly back and forth in rhythm to her stroking tongue.

The cornfield buzzed, the sun glared.

Susan gasped, a shiver coursing the full length of her bent body, Eva finding and flailing the woman's engorged clit with her tongue. Susan urgently spread Eva's pussy lips and propped the woman's swollen clit up with her fingers, sucked it into her mouth. Eva quivered uncontrollably.

The two women came in one another's mouths, all over each other's faces, absolutely gushing their joy.

Proving to the both of them once and for all just how unpredictable and exciting police work really can be.

Personal Shopper
by Viva Jones

'Do you think the rose or the peach suits me better?' Sam asked, holding two pastel-coloured chiffon blouses up against her skin.

'With your colouring, both actually work really well,' Claire asserted. 'But the peach goes better with that suit, if that's what you were thinking about wearing it with.'

'It's such a smart bloody weekend I don't know what to do.' Sam sighed, putting the blouses down and having a sip of the chilled champagne that was a private customer's privilege. 'All I know is that I need five or six different outfits, including two evening dresses. Oh God, I wish I didn't have to go.'

'Look, this skirt's gorgeous, and there's some peach there, you see, in the pattern, and that would pick out the blouse nicely.'

Claire was a personal shopper, who had set up her own boutique in one of the smartest areas in London. She loved being in daily contact with people, loved pleasing her customers and had a keen eye for what worked or didn't work on a person – she was also sensitive enough to nudge them away from designer disasters and towards style success without hurting their feelings. To this day she was amazed at how witless many hot, successful and well-married women were about the clothes that worked with their colouring and body shapes. Sam was her ideal customer: beautiful, slim and entirely out of her depth with haute couture. She also had an extremely rich fiancé willing to pick up the bill.

Claire watched as, without a hint of self-consciousness, Sam unzipped the skinny jeans she was wearing and tore off her white blouse to reveal a slim, toned and olive-skinned body that wouldn't have looked out of place in a swimwear catalogue.

'So you're getting married, then?' Claire asked as she tried not to stare too much. She was used to what she politely called "rangier" physiques, belonging to corporate wives who'd spent too many years entertaining for their own good.

'This is the engagement weekend,' Sam told her. 'At his parents' manor house somewhere in the heart of Gloucester. All their friends will be there,' she added, pulling on the skirt and zipping it up. 'And most of them are titled. It's going to be a total bloody nightmare.'

'Why do you say that?'

'Look at me. My parents run a grocer's in Hendon. I'm a scholarship girl. I mean, I love Tim and all that, really I do. The minute I met him I knew he was the one for me, I just had no idea his family were so loaded, or so up themselves, to be honest with you. They don't want Indian blood running in their heirs' veins, I know they don't.' She studied herself in the mirror critically. 'Is this too big for me?'

'Let me have a look.' Claire stepped forward and slipped her hand inside the waistband. 'You want a little room, don't you? For all those six-course banquets, I mean.'

The two women giggled and Claire could see Sam beginning to relax. 'I could get you a smaller size if you like?'

'Let me just try it with the blouse first.'

Sam pulled it on and arranged it thoughtfully. 'You're so right, it totally works. It says "respectable and chic". It says I know how to behave myself in smart company. I like that.' She smiled wryly, before having another large gulp of champagne. 'Aren't you having any?'

'No, it's only there for customers.'

'Oh come off it, you can't let me drink alone!' Sam insisted, reaching forward to pour Claire a glass. 'And you know what they say, the customer's always right.'

They clinked glasses. 'Of course they are,' Claire agreed. 'And I'll do anything to please my customers.'

'OK, now it's time for evening wear,' Sam said, putting her glass down. 'Formal and elegant, more Audrey Hepburn than Liz Hurley, if you get my drift.'

'How about this one?' Claire reached for a sea-blue asymmetrical dress that was split up to the thigh.

'Oh, no, that is *so* Liz Hurley!' Sam laughed. 'I've got to be more covered up than that!'

'Why, exactly?' Claire asked. 'You've got beautiful skin, and a fabulous body, why not flaunt it?'

'Tim's parents wouldn't approve, I just know it.' Sam took another swig of champagne.

'It's not his parents you're marrying, is it? Why don't you just try it on?'

Sam looked tempted. 'It's so not going to work, but I do like it!' she said with a giggle, and began to unbutton the blouse.

As she did so, Claire felt a pang of desire. Sam's skin was smooth and caramel-coloured and smelt faintly of rose oil. For a second Claire longed to catch a glimpse of her breasts. She watched as Sam casually unzipped the skirt and let it drop to the floor. Claire picked both items up and hung them back on the rack.

'Wow, you're so tidy, could you move in with me once we're married? I'm terrible that way!'

The two women laughed as Sam started stepping into the dress. Then, realising that her bra wouldn't work, she unclasped it and threw it onto a chair, revealing two perfect, small, round breasts with dark nipples. 'Now, how does this fasten?'

Claire helped her to fasten the dress, which hung from one shoulder, and as her fingers brushed against Sam's skin, she felt that flash of desire again. Normally she went for men, but every now and then there'd been a girl who'd turned her world upside down, a girl whose pussy she couldn't get enough of, a girl whose taste and feel and touch were never far from her mind. And once again she could feel that longing, that desire, for Sam.

Claire stood back to admire her customer's reflection in the mirror. 'That looks fabulous, absolutely stunning, but then you'd look great in a bin bag.'

Sam was admiring herself from all angles. 'It does, doesn't it? Is the split very high?' She parted her legs, trying to see if she might reveal too much, and Claire caught a glimpse of the pink silk and lace knickers she was wearing underneath, and she longed to pull the fabric to one side and take a peek at what was hiding underneath.

'I think you can get away with it.'

'What would Tim think?'

'That he was marrying the most knock-out woman in London. You look amazing.'

Sam smiled, showing a spark of rebellion. 'OK, let's go for it. That and the other two on the "yes" pile,' she decided, stepping out of the dress and sipping more champagne, unselfconsciously wearing nothing but her knickers. 'I like your top, by the way,' she said, admiring Claire's sleeveless pink blouse.

Claire giggled. 'My naughty secret. It's actually from Primark, but don't tell anyone.'

'You're kidding! But it's so well made, I mean the stitching and everything.' Sam stepped forward and touched the fabric where it framed Claire's breast and, as she stroked it, once again, Claire felt that flash of desire between her legs and longed to touch Sam's naked breasts, whose nipples were now quite hard. She wondered what they'd feel like against her lips – hard little Tic Tacs, perhaps, or sweet M&M's? For a second their eyes met, and each could sense a reciprocal pang of desire.

'I'm sorry, maybe I've had too much champagne,' Sam hiccupped, stepping back.

The moment was gone. Claire reached for more clothes for her customer to try on, more luxurious colours and fabrics, and quietly admired Sam's body as she stepped in and out of them. Everything looked superb on her, and as she gently pushed Sam towards the more revealing pieces, she couldn't help but envy Tim for having this girl all to himself.

'OK, that's the "yes" pile, and over there are the "nos",'

Sam declared once she'd tried most of the clothing on. With every decision they'd had a celebratory sip of champagne, and were in good spirits. Sam was now wearing a shimmering silver evening gown, cut on the bias, which was just a little too big for her breasts. 'I really like this one,' she said sadly, tugging up the material. 'Can we take it in?'

'I think that's possible,' Claire told her, reaching for some pins. She pulled Sam round straight so that she could examine it properly and, as she tweaked the fabric here and there, her fingers brushed lightly against Sam's breasts. 'Just here, and here,' she said, trying to concentrate on the material. 'What do you think?'

Sam looked at herself in the mirror. 'That's better. Wow. I look like a princess.' With a giggle, she reached over and collected their glasses, insisting that Claire have a sip more. 'You've got such a good eye, you know that? You seem to understand me and my body far better than I do. It's as if you've known me for ages.'

'I really enjoy matching the right clothes to the right person,' Claire admitted, unzipping the back of Sam's dress, and fighting off the thoughts of how much better she'd like to get to know Sam's body. 'It gives me a lot of satisfaction. And you've got such an amazing figure that everything looks fantastic on you.'

'You think so?' Sam looked reflective. 'Tim's not big on compliments, so I never know. He wishes I could be more adventurous. At first he liked that I was this prim girl with an Indian mum, but sometimes I get the impression ...' Her voice trailed off.

'That what?'

'I don't know. That I should be more experienced. You know, I've only ever slept with him. He's all I've ever known. And he thinks I'm inhibited by his parents, which I suppose is true, and that I shouldn't care what people think. And then the other day he said I should get a breast enlargement!'

'No! You have perfect breasts. What's he talking about?'

More than ever, Claire was overwhelmed with a desire to cup Sam's boobs, to feel the hardness of her nipples and to feel

39

their weight in her hands. As if reading her mind, Sam reached out and, very matter-of-factly, took Claire's hands and placed them on her breasts. Claire looked at her, unsure what to do next, and gently started to massage them, playing with the nipples between her thumbs and forefingers.

'I think they're perfect,' she whispered.

She carried on stroking them, relishing the smoothness of Sam's skin, and the hard nubs of her nipples. Then she couldn't help herself, and dropped down to take one in her mouth, to lick and suck and tease and to taste how perfect they were for herself. She heard Sam sigh and throw her head back, and saw how her shiny long hair cascaded down her back. God, how she wanted this woman!

Suddenly Sam leant forward, cupping her hands around Claire's face, and pulled her up towards her. Then they came together in an urgent, hungry union, kissing and licking and running their hands over each other's bodies. Sam's hands stroked Claire's back, urging down the zip of her top. Claire pulled back to help her, yanking it off over her head.

'You're so beautiful,' Sam gasped.

She reached around Claire's back and unfastened her bra, then pulled it off and tossed it onto the floor. Then she stroked her pale, firm breasts, slightly fuller and rounder than her own, and teased her nipples with her fingers. She dropped down and took one, then the other, in her mouth, licking and biting and sucking them.

'I've never done anything like this before,' she whispered after a while. 'But now I have, I love how it feels,' she added, moving upwards to kiss Claire's neck and breathe in the warmth of her scent. Their lips found each other again and locked in another deep kiss, their tongues exploring and probing, both delighting in each other's softness and femininity. 'I always wondered what it was like for a man, you know, to feel a girl's tits, and now I know,' Sam said breathlessly. 'And it's so lovely, I'm almost jealous.'

'He's crazy if he thinks yours are too small,' Claire told her before they kissed again, and continued to play with each other's breasts. 'He needs his head examined.'

'And he was grumbling about my bush,' Sam admitted with a giggle. 'So I had my first Brazilian yesterday.'

'You did?' Claire asked, wondering if, and hoping, this was an invitation. She ran her hands over her customer's body, feeling the flatness of her stomach, before she let her fingers slide down into her knickers, where she stroked the small strip of perfectly manicured hair.

'It feels good to me,' she said, and then, wondering if she'd gone too far, pulled her hand out quickly again. 'I'm sorry. I don't know what got into me.'

'God, no, don't worry about it. Do it again. I mean, Tim's always telling me to be less conservative. I want to touch you there too. In fact, I just want to totally make love to you. Let's face it, if I'm about to get married, I'd better have my one lesbian experience before it happens,' she added, a defiant and excited glint in her eyes. She then tugged at Claire's skirt, unbuttoning it and forcing the zip down until it dropped to the floor. Now they were both naked apart from their knickers.

'Let me do what you just did.' Sam slipped her hand inside Claire's knickers to feel her bush. Claire did the same, and they fell together again in a kiss, or many wet, slippery, kisses, mirroring each other, slipping their hands down each other's knickers, feeling the newly-clipped strips of hair, before slowly slipping their fingers down deeper. Both delved down into each other's pussy, gently prising open the folds beneath. Sam was bolder; she let her finger go further, until it was immersed in Claire's wetness. Then she pulled it out and put it between their lips, and they kissed and licked the moistness together.

Claire now manoeuvred Sam to the elegant Regency chair on which guest shoppers were invited to sit, and Sam opened her legs wide. Claire knelt down in front of her and gently pulled the expensive fabric of Sam's knickers away from her pussy. She stopped to admire how beautiful it looked, so clean and smooth and tempting. Then she buried her tongue down there, exploring the folds and contours, imagining that Sam's soft flesh was the gentlest, most luxurious swathes of fabric enveloping her: the finest silks and cashmeres in shades of creamy coffee and pink, and that she was gradually parting

41

them to reveal a warm moist tunnel within.

'Oh, God, wait,' Sam gasped. 'Let me take these off.' She got up and wriggled out of her moist knickers. 'You've made me so wet. Now let's try again.' She sat down again, but this time lifted her leg up on one side of the chair, so that Claire could fully appreciate the beauty of her cunt. Once again, she enveloped herself in Sam's luxuriously soft folds, from licking the nub of her clitoris to darting down and pressing her tongue deep inside the moist tunnel of her pussy.

'Oh God, stop,' Sam urged. 'I'm going to come, and it's too soon. I need to eat you too,' she told Claire, urging her to stand up. Then she pulled down her knickers and let Claire step out of them. Next, holding Claire's hips, she leant forward and dipped her tongue into Claire's pussy, urging it deeper and deeper, further into her folds, all the time staring up at Claire with her big brown eyes. 'You taste amazing,' she whispered, her lips glossy with Claire's juices. 'But I can't get enough.'

She slid off the chair and onto the carpet, where Claire followed her lead, sinking down onto her knees. Sam pushed her back and then climbed on top, so that her tongue easily reached Claire's pussy, and her own pussy was positioned perfectly above Claire's face.

For someone who'd never been with a girl before, Claire thought, Sam was a complete natural, as together they licked and kissed, explored and savoured each other, delighting in their softness, their smoothness and the luxury of the delicate skin they were tasting.

Then Sam pulled herself over and opened her legs wide, allowing Claire to do the same, so that they were lying side by side, and each could admire and taste the extent of the other's cunts and arses, probing with tongues and fingers, mirroring one another. Following each other's lead, they pulled open their pussy lips wide and sucked on their clits; they sank two fingers inside their cunts, rubbing their clits with their thumbs. They darted their tongues deep up to their butts, exploring the crinkly skin there, and they lavishly licked each other's clits until Sam went first, exploding into deep, muscular spasms of orgasm that sent her thrashing on the floor, crying and yelping and screaming so that Claire had to struggle to keep her tongue firmly on her pussy.

'Oh my God, that was so amazing, that was just the best.' She stroked Claire's hair tenderly. 'You're amazing, you know that? And now I'm going to give you the biggest orgasm you've ever had in your life. How d'you want it?'

Claire straddled Sam's face, balancing on her knees, and looked to the heavens – or at least the chandelier – while Sam's tongue built up a steady rhythm against her clit, urging her to come. She manoeuvred her thumb inside Claire and pressed it deep, while stroking her butt with her middle finger. All Sam could think of was Claire's sweet pinkness, and the juices that were now flooding over her face. As Claire's orgasm built up, so Sam kept up the pressure, until finally Claire burst like a dam, unleashing torrents of water from her body and her being. As she writhed and thrashed, Sam did her best to cling on to her pussy, like a piece of timber being swept away in the flow. When Claire's flood finally subsided, she fell on the carpet beside her, and they held each other's limp, wasted bodies, and fell into a slight but satisfying slumber.

Half an hour later, as Sam lay snoozing, Claire got up, washed herself quickly in the bathroom, dressed and began packing up Sam's weekend clothes. Making sure her customer couldn't hear, she dialled her financial backer.

'It's me. If you've got your credit card, I can give you the details now … Yes, I did what you asked, and pushed her away from the prudish things … She has no idea how stunning she is … Well, maybe she does now … Oh, and she thinks your parents aren't keen, so you'll have to put her straight there …'

At the sight of Sam, now dressed and cleaned up, Claire became more formal.

'That's great, yes, and if there are any problems, you can have a full refund, no question.' She put the phone down.

'Tim?' Sam asked.

'He just settled the bill.'

'You know, weirdly, I don't think he'd mind–'

'He adores you. And you're going to be very happy.'

'Yes.' Sam smiled in relief. 'We are. But, you know, I love what just happened between us. I feel it's sort of opened me up, like I'm willing to try more with him now. Maybe I have been a bit missionary position in the past?' Suddenly her eyes lit up and she smiled at Claire in complicity. 'Would you do honeymoon clothes, by any chance? You know, Tim's chartering a yacht, and I haven't got a thing to wear.'

'Sailing outfits? Sarongs? Bikinis?' Claire smiled back. 'You try to stop me.' She handed Sam the bags. 'Like I always say, anything to please my customers.'

Stick Garden
by Sommer Marsden

'What in the world is this?' I couldn't keep the laughter out of my voice even as Maddy frowned.

'It will be a garden.'

'What kind? A stick garden?'

She stood, deep red hair – the colour of Japanese maple leaves in autumn – swaying with the movement. 'No. Right now is the fall planting. There'll be vines, vegetables, tomato bushes and corn come the summer ...'

'And on her farm she had some sticks ...' I teased, singing in my best Southern accent.

Maddy swatted my ass with her slender but fast hand and I yelped. 'Enough of that, Nina, or no reaping of the goods for you.'

'But I live to reap,' I said and winked.

I teased her all through dinner about the stakes she'd driven into that large bare patch out back. She'd driven them down and tilled the soil and the whole thing was lit by marvellous moonlight by the time we went to bed.

I fell asleep fast. We live out in the middle of nowhere. A mile to the nearest house. There's hardly any noise out there at all, especially in the fall when the tourists head back to the cities.

She had the silk scarf knotted in the centre so the knot rested in my mouth like a ball gag. She tied it on me before I was even really awake. 'What are you doing?' I asked, but of course it was muffled and she had no idea what I was saying.

'Come on then, Miss Smarty Pants,' Maddy said in her no-nonsense way. She rarely raised her voice or showed high emotion. It was all about how quiet Maddy got. The more upset she was, the softer her voice. 'We'll show you the power of a garden.'

I fought but only for a second. I'd had nothing to do with bondage or submission or any of it before Maddy. But she saw something in me and the first time she told me to lie across her lap my world had changed. She marched me downstairs and I barely kept up with her in my tired stumbling steps.

'You shouldn't poke fun of things that will nourish you,' she told me sternly. My neck flared with goosebumps as my brain kicked into gear and I realised she was leading me out back. And I was naked.

'You've got a quick tongue, but how about my hard work? How about the teasing? How about the food that will feed you when harvest time comes?'

I shook my head. I had no way to say I was sorry. I had no way to tell her I hadn't realised how important it all was. But I knew deep down that she was about to extract her apology from my body. She would make me pay. And then she would reward me for my courage.

Two things happened simultaneously. My stomach buzzed with nervous energy and a hint of fear, and my pussy went wet and soft.

'What you need is some perspective. Let's take you out to the *stick* garden,' she said, and I shook with the chill of the fall night.

I put the brakes on and dug my heels into the soft earth. I could smell the dirt that she'd just turned and the moist scent of dew on greens. I could smell the autumn leaves beginning their breakdown cycle so everything smelt musky and rich. I dug my heels in and stared up at the fat white moon and shook my head. No.

It was a mistake, I knew it. But her small hand – so fucking small you'd never guess it powerful or wicked – landed on my ass and the crack reached my ears before the pain truly registered. But it did register and a searing heat lit up my right ass cheek like a flame was licking at my skin.

'Did you just tell me no?'

I blinked, tears prickling the inner edges of my eyes. My nipples stood out hard, cold and yet excited by the whole scenario. Teased erect by air and intent and lust for this woman.

I shook my head no again.

'I didn't think so.' She prodded me with her knee to the back of mine and I let her guide me dead centre into a white stain of moonlight. Maddy turned me and whispered against my neck 'Put your arms out, brat.' She kissed me hard even as my arms flew out to my sides in my obedience.

'Good. That's better.'

With a leather thong she took from her pocket, she tied first one wrist and then the other. I stood spreadeagled in the garden, each arm bound to one of her stakes. Maddy stepped back to stare and I realised how unbelievably bright the moon was. It was like a small spotlight on our little scene.

'What a pretty scarecrow,' she whispered and stepped forward to run her hand up the inside of one thigh before moving to the other. I shook as if I had a fever. I prayed she'd touch me where I needed it most.

I moved my hips just a bit, hoping against hope she wouldn't notice.

Maddy laughed and my heart jumped. 'Now did you think I wouldn't pick up on that little twist of the hips, Nina-pie? Bad, bad girl.' The swat to my ass landed and my back bowed briefly with the force of the blow. She was small, but she was a badass.

I shook my head no again. Maddy had taken my power of speech. More than ever I was at her mercy, bound out here and gagged. No way to call for help, not that help was anywhere near our house on any given day. The thought of being under her small talented thumb made my cunt flex with anticipation. I shut my eyes and said a prayer for relief. A touch, a kiss, a stroke.

Instead I got the sharp feel of a stick running the back of my leg as Maddy paced around me. 'You need to realise out here in the garden, that under the sun the plant will find warmth and light, and it will flourish.'

Maddy ran her hand over my hair, stroking me like a cat. Petting me. I shut my eyes to soak in the sensation of her gentle touch. Her hand slid down my neck, brushing my shoulders with a lulling attention. I sighed against the knotted scarf, letting her touch me however she wanted. The point is that she was doing it at all.

She traced the curve of my spine, ticking off each knob of bone until she hit my lower back and then palmed my bottom. I forced my body to be still. I forced my mind to stay unfocused and malleable. From behind, she slipped her finger into my pussy, even as her other hand guided the stick she held to scratch along my lower calf. The two sensations together confused my body – kept me off balance.

Her hand fell away and I sighed, moving like a leaf in the wind. I tossed and turned gently in my bonds, hoping against hope for more contact. Maddy clucked her tongue as she came into view; she shook her head and said, 'Try and behave, girl.'

I shivered seeing the glint in her eye. I knew that look. I nodded; my only recourse.

'When the rain comes,' she said, tracing the inside of my legs with that damn stick – a nod to my bratty comment about her stick garden, 'it will help the plant stay … moist.'

The stick hit the fragile skin at the top of my thigh. She gave it a good whack and the flesh let loose a spark of pain. But my pussy went wet all the same, a magical process. The sharp bite of pain and then the pleasure bleeding in right behind it. The first time Maddy had spanked me, I'd laughed and cried simultaneously and then had simply gone boneless when she fucked me to orgasm with her fingers.

Whack, whack, whack went the stick and my heart lodged firmly in my throat as I tried so hard to breathe and not weep.

'The plant will get sun and get water. The plant will grow.' *Whack.*

'The plant will twine around these sticks, as you call them, and the plant will thrive.' *Whack.*

'The garden will not be a barren patch full of stakes and

furrows and naked dirt. It will be green and lush.' *Whack*.

'It will be sexy and abundant.' *Whack*.

I found myself nodding with her lecture. Nodding like a mindless, desperate bobblehead as she preached to me for putting down a garden she had clearly thought out, adored and worked to bring into reality. For *us*.

'It's for me and you, Nina, a gift to our home. A source of nourishment. Something we'll work together – as a couple. The woman I love and hard work out in the sunshine.' *Whack, whack, whack …* She alternated, hitting the top of one thigh and then the other, but never ever hitting my clit. Never ever stroking it or even smacking it. She left welts that I could feel riding the tops of my legs like ridges of heat along my skin.

Maddy dropped the stick and my blood leapt. I tried to breathe but the adrenaline in my body was filling my veins, shutting down my logical thoughts. I trembled and the wind blew hard to lick at my naked illuminated skin.

She ripped the scarf from my lips and stepped in closer, toe to toe, face to face, barely an inch between us. 'Say you're sorry.'

'I'm sorry, baby. So sorry.'

'Were you bad?'

'I was bad.'

'Will you work hard in our garden? The one I've wished for us since we bought this land?'

I nodded, in my head demanding she kiss me, forgive me, touch me. 'I will. I will work hard with you. And then I'll cook our food and we'll eat and we'll can vegetables and we'll …' I trailed off, losing track of my own babble.

'Tell me you love me,' Maddy said, her dark eyes darker in the moonlight. Her red hair nearly black in the silver air.

Oh that was easy. 'I love you, I love you, baby.'

She nodded. 'Good.' Then she pushed the knotted scarf back past my lips and smiled. 'To keep you quiet.'

When she dropped to her knees I did weep, tears streaking hot lines down my cold face. Her mouth found me, her lips pressed my pussy lips. Her scalding little tongue found my clit and she pressed hard with just the tip. Then with broad flat licks she brought me close, right to the edge. Maddy stopped, laughing hard. 'Not so fast, smartass.' She held me still with her strong little hands.

Her fingers tickled over the welts she'd created. She pressed the fragile skin until I shimmered under her. I tried to pull away and she bit one welt just hard enough that a rush of fluid slid from my pussy. 'Does that hurt?' she asked, as if she didn't know.

I nodded, blips of pain firing off under my skin. She moved so that her hand slipped inside me. Fingers pressed deep into my cunt, curling in a come-hither gesture and my knees sagged. Cold and weak and tethered, I mumbled under the gag, *Pleasepleaseplease …*

Maddy took pity on me. Pressed her lips back to me, licking me in silverfish darts as her fingers delved deeper, nudged my G-spot and I sighed.

'Come on now. Come for Mamma.'

She nipped my clit and the waterfall of pain did me in. I came with a muffled cry that had her chuckling in the sterling moonlight.

I gripped the stakes with a death grip until she pried me loose – finger by finger. She yanked the gag free. 'Come on now. Let go so we can get inside.'

'Inside?'

'You're going to get on your knees for me,' she said. 'Finish making this up to me.'

'Yes, ma'am.'

'Such a good girl,' she said and picked up her stick.

Waiting for Isabella
by Amy Eddison

From the moment I'd taken her call I'd been in a state of nervous anticipation. Her voice had the mildest accent, throaty and alluring and her name – Isabella – rolled off her tongue as I wrote it in my diary. It was supposed to have been my first day off for over two weeks, and I hadn't booked anyone else in, but when she'd rung me at 10 a.m., and I'd just finished giving myself the first of many orgasms that day, her irresistible voice had me hot and unable to say no.

It must have been a full moon, I thought to myself after orgasm number three in the shower; I always became like a dog on heat at a full moon, though a month of hard work and no play also meant that I'd been lacking in the bedroom department.

After a light dinner, I dressed in my normal working gear – some tight leggings and a vest top; the temperature in the therapy room had to be kept high, but I was always hot after working hard so clothes were always minimal but not overtly revealing. Normally the underwear was simple too, but I found my hands picking out the set I normally saved for nights out in a club, when the ladies were ready for action and anything could happen. I looked at myself in the mirror. I'd been neglecting my appearance since beginning to work from home, but my toned muscles were giving my body a nice shape and my perky little tits sat nicely in the lacy balcony bra. I turned to see how the rest of me was doing from all the hard work and the new running regime I'd begun. My legs looked pretty good, pale but smooth and blemish free, and I couldn't help thinking that my rear looked damn cute in the little thong, worked into shape from the rhythmical rocking required by the Thai massage I loved to perform. Anyway, the exotic lady about to arrive wanted a Swedish massage; warm oil rubbed all over her body – perfect for a late-night booking after a day of tending to my own needs for a change …

The new DVD I'd ordered from an American erotica company was hotter and heavier than any I'd seen before and the ladies on there had been gorgeous; more than enough for my imagination to run wild as I played with my pussy. One lady in particular – a dominatrix – had got me lurching around on the living room floor as she treated the little blonde with her like a toy – ordering her about in her little pink dress as the PVC-clad dominatrix spanked her and tied her to the wall. She was stunning. When she'd finished her fun and stepped out of her corset and mask, she'd been exactly as I'd imagined Isabella to look. Dark and sultry with femininity added to her kinkiness. I could hope …

Finally, as I ran a brush through my long blonde hair and then tied it loosely in a ponytail to the side, the doorbell rang.

'Isabella?' I enquired, knowing it must be her.

'Hi, Rose, thanks so much for fitting me in at short notice – I can't tell you what pain I'm in.' She breezed into the flat and I led her through to my therapy room, trying to keep my excitement hidden. She was perfect. A dominatrix in the making. I inwardly shivered as a little wave of excitement began building again in my clit.

'Come in.' I smiled and her eyes met mine; they were friendly, open and dreamily dark. 'So, what's the problem? Your shoulders, you mentioned,' I said and immediately she slipped off her jacket and let her silk top fall off her delicate shoulder.

'Right here,' she said, indicating a visible lump in her right shoulder, just below her neck. 'It hurts so much I haven't slept for days.' Pain hung in her big dark eyes.

I walked over and took hold of her slender shoulders and could feel heat rising from the mass of knots. I slowly began to work my fingers into it, knowing exactly what I needed to do.

'Can you fill this form in for me please?' I said and left her to fill in her details while I impulsively lit all the candles in the room. It had turned from dusk into full darkness during my last appointment and I suddenly wanted this woman to have the most relaxing and indulgent treatment possible. I mixed up a little oil, using rose, geranium and jasmine, then sneaking a glance at my new, unbelievably arousing client I added a few drops of patchouli: the most sensual oil of them all.

'Thanks, I'll leave you to get undressed, and I'll be back in a mo ...' She had already slid off her top, revealing a stunning pale pink and lemon silk bra – a perfect match against her olive skin.

'Oh, don't worry, I'm not shy,' she said and her smile creased the curve of her cheek to reveal perfect little dimples. She pulled off her pencil skirt, gliding it over her ample hips and I could see her underwear was perfectly matching and her body quite simply the most perfect thing I'd ever seen. 'Face down?' she asked as she unclasped her bra and glided it down her arms, throwing the exquisite item idly onto the chair. I nodded, stunned silent and eager to get my hands onto her body.

'Hmmm,' she murmured with the first stroke of my hands up her back, close to her spine. I did several repetitions of the stroke, deep and hard, until her back couldn't help but relax. After some kneading and strong stroking of her entire back, it was nice and warm, and ready for me to get deep.

'Is the pressure OK for you?' I asked as I went to re-oil my hands with the heavenly scented oil, now filling the room with its powerful and arousing aroma.

'Absolutely perfect.' She spoke lazily now and I knew the hard part – the actually getting the client to let go and relax part – was over. 'I think I've just died and gone to heaven.'

I couldn't help feeling the same as I moved to stand at her head. Her shiny hair was in tousled curls, which she'd carelessly piled on top of her head and it was gleaming with health. I slowly kneaded into the offending knots and, as I felt the muscles begin to relax, I used my elbow to swiftly push them along her scapula. There was an almighty clunk as her shoulder fell back into its natural position and the knot disappeared.

'Sorry,' I said, worry rising in me, hoping I hadn't hurt her too much.

'No pain, no gain,' was her only response in her soft and lightly accented voice.

Still, I wanted to soothe her after the pain and began to work downwards, gazing at the perfect curve of her lower back, spreading out to reveal the sensuous mound of her cheeks, outlined by the pink and lemon silk thong, just peeking out from the towel that I'd somehow left far lower than I ever usually did.

All thoughts of my bath and a good book disappeared and my whole world became this woman's body as I worked. The music was ideal for drifting away and, as a light purr of a snore began to sound, I knew Isabella was right wherever she wanted to be. I was beginning my own dream as I eased the tension out of her muscles and gazed at her beauty and I hoped she was somewhere similar. It had been a long time since I'd been this close to a woman as beautiful as her and it was the only place I wanted to be.

Her lower back revealed some crunches too, so I began slowly to work into her hips. My fingers eased around her coccyx and into each buttock where I found knots of tension that needed to go. I didn't want to shock her, so I whispered, 'This may be a little sore.'

'Whatever you have to do ...' she said. I was pleased she had so much trust in me, and also that I knew she wasn't totally out for the count. I slowly introduced my elbow to her behind and then forced it deeper, circling around inside each cheek until every crunch was gone and I could feel her come back to life. 'That feels amazing.'

'It's a Thai massage technique – excellent for opening up the hips,' I told her; though I could think of other ways to open her up, I kept them to myself and went back to stroking her rhythmically, soothing the muscles I'd just forced my way into.

'I love Thailand. I spent a year there when I was writing my last book,' she said. 'It was the best year of my life; I almost didn't come back.' I was very glad she had.

'That must have been incredible. Whereabouts were you?' I asked as I moved down to her right leg and took a glance at her personal details. Occupation: Writer. Next of Kin: Rafael Russo. Damn; same surname, must be a husband. My excitement began to wane.

'I travelled about a lot, saw most of it, I guess. A beautiful, sensual place, and such amazing people.' We continued to share our experiences of Thailand and found we had been to many of the same places and had very much the same overwhelming love for the place and its people. The conversation flowed and the pleasure I was getting from giving her the pleasure she voiced throughout was enough to mean 90 minutes had passed before I even looked at the clock. Overrunning by 30 minutes was not something I made a habit of, and I was almost embarrassed to tell her.

'That's fine. I needed it and I'm happy to pay extra.' Unfortunately she didn't mean extra in the way many of the sleazy men who called me in the middle of the night meant.

I was right at the end, having noticed a lack of any rings, when I finally asked about her writing. 'Oh I write erotica,' she said and our eyes met as I felt my cheeks glow, perhaps with a mild embarrassment, but then I was no prude. No, it was the dampness the words had instantly produced in my own silky thong that had me hot. Her eyes didn't leave mine as I made the final strokes to her gorgeous face and then told her I was done.

'I'll let you get dressed now,' I told her, but her hand reached out to grab me – not that I was putting up any resistance.

'Don't leave,' she said and suddenly words weren't necessary; her eyes said it all. I bent down to kiss her plump and now glistening mouth and her arm wound around my neck, holding me close to her as her mouth opened to take in my tongue. 'I think it's my turn now. You must need a massage as well after all that hard work!' She slowly got off the bed and pulled off my vest top to reveal my perky tits, sitting in the tight lace. She stroked my chest, reaching inside to cup my breast and my nipple instantly hardened. She expertly unclasped the bra and let it fall to the floor before she took each nipple in turn into her warm mouth. I was gasping with delight before she even took off my leggings. She eased herself onto the floor, her butt cheeks spreading below her in all their glory as she crouched down on her knees and slid the obstructing article down my legs, leaving only my thong.

'Onto the bed then.' She giggled delightedly as her fingers flicked lightly against my clit and then she spanked me, seemingly enjoying the wobble that ran through my derriere. I climbed onto the bed and lay where she had just left. I could smell the oil as she spread it liberally over my back, but mixed with it was the scent of her. A delicious scent that was arousing me more and more as she got closer to my head, mimicking the moves I'd made on her. She was good – too good. I could feel myself relaxing but I didn't want the sexual tension to go. As though she'd read my mind, her soft hands glided down to my thonged behind and, without any of the professionalism I'd shown, went straight under the thong and rubbed at my anus with her oiled fingers. I clenched in shock but also in delight.

'Hmm, you like that, do you?' She edged a finger into my anus and it rose up to meet her, leaving a gap for her hand to get underneath me. I slid my torso down a little, raising my ass in the air so her entire arm was under me, her fingers stroking my clit as her arm pushed into my opening. She slid in and out of me, into my pussy, opening it wider with every move, and then her finger slid back to go further into my open and ready anus.

'Oh my God!' I shouted out, warning her that I was close to the edge and she took her arm away, only to slap my quivering ass cheeks again and again until they stung.

'Turn over please,' she instructed and I couldn't move fast enough. She slid her own oily body onto mine and we fitted together perfectly. Her large breasts pressed against my own smaller ones and we kissed with more passion than I'd ever before possessed. She licked me like a cat, on my lips, and into my mouth, her moist tongue teasing me and then she moved down, lapping at my neck, sucking it and blowing on it, and

sending shivers down my spine as I writhed underneath h.
wrapping my legs around her womanly hips and pulling hei
pussy into mine. Then she reached her arm round to push my
legs away and somehow managed to turn herself 90 degrees so
that her gorgeous and already glistening pussy was directly
above my face.

My tongue went to work on her as hers did on me, and then
all mental capacities broke down as our animalistic instincts
took over and we lapped at each other's pussies, tasting,
pressing and delving deeper and deeper. As her finger re-
entered my anus, my arm reached around to her tight little hole,
and she moaned with delight as we writhed into one another
until an almighty orgasm erupted through the both of us. She
wriggled around so her head was back next to mine and she
snuggled against my chest as it continued to heave and my
breath slowly slowed down to normal.

'That was without a doubt the best massage I've ever had.
Thank you so much. I think I'll have to begin coming
regularly ... is that what you'd recommend?' She gazed up at
me, a glint in her eye.

'I think you need to come daily, Isabella. At least once,' I
replied and my hand began to slowly stroke her perfect breast
into renewed excitement. This time, I was going to take the
lead. I slid from underneath her and suggested I go and pour us
a glass of the champagne that had been waiting in my fridge for
such an occasion.

'Purrrrfect,' she said.

I went into the bedroom and got what I needed from my
play box: a pair of pink furry cuffs and my favourite vibrator. I
laid them on my four-poster and then went to open the
champagne.

'Mind if I use the bathroom?' Isabella emerged, still
completely naked and I gazed with adoration as she strode
across the kitchen in all her voluptuous glory.

'It's through there.' I pointed and continued to watch her.

'In here,' I called from the bedroom as she called my name
a few minutes later.

'This is a beautiful flat, Rose. You have some seriously

good taste,' she said as she looked around my bedroom. Adorned with erotic artwork from every era, her eyes fell on my particular favourite: a modern photographic print of a perfectly formed specimen of womanly beauty, curled up on a bed, her hands between her legs, with satin and silk falling all around her. It was far from explicit, but there was something I found incredibly arousing about it, and seemingly Isabella did too.

'Come here,' I said, in a voice of authority. She smiled as I saw her notice my toys. She sat beside me and I handed her a glass of champagne, which she drank hungrily. I took my own glass and downed it in one then poured us some more. Immediately I took her wrists and carefully cuffed them to the bedpost, making sure she was comfortable as I made her helpless. Her legs were open in anticipation, but she still showed shock as I dribbled the cold bubbles onto her warmth, licking slowly; I simply wanted to make sure she was wet and ready. Then I turned on the vibrator and, beginning at her toes, I glided it slowly up her body, missing out her pussy to begin with; I wanted every inch of her to enjoy the tingling pleasure. Her legs began to writhe around on the satin bedspread and I forced them down, moving my body weight on top of her. I could see myself in the mirror at the foot of my bed – a pleasure I'd always enjoyed; the sight of myself giving pleasure had me feeling a renewed urgency. I slid the vibrator to her clit and she let out a sharp moan. I quickly moved to her opening and spread her lips with one hand as the other forced the vibrator inside. Her eyes opened wide as her pussy consumed it and I began to push it in and out, deeper and deeper, before withdrawing and lightly touching her clit again, before forcing into her. She was gasping and panting when I suddenly took it out and placed it in my mouth, licking up her juices. She moaned again, watching as I spread my own pussy wide, kneeling on the bed with my legs at either side of her. I watched her watch it enter my dripping pussy and almost came instantly. I took it out swiftly and pushed it into her waiting mouth so she could lick and suck it, as I knew she would.

Then I showed her the main benefit of my special toy. I put

it back into her, then moved myself up to wrap my legs around her hips and sunk myself down onto her so that we were fucking the same dripping, vibrating sex toy. 'Fuck, fuck, fuck …' Isabella began to cry and I felt myself approaching the edge. 'I'm going to …' We both exploded at the same time as our pelvises ground into one another.

It was a while before either of us spoke as we let our breath catch up. 'I've written about you before. You were a vision that came to me in my wildest fantasies, but I think I always knew I'd find you in the flesh one day,' Isabella murmured as she fell into a deep sleep in my arms.

The Trip of a Lifetime
by Izzy French

'Charles Street,' Claudia gasped, dropping into the seat, throwing her bag to the floor. The driver nodded. A woman, Claudia noticed. That was a relief. She'd had her fill of men for now. And she had a nice welcoming smile.

'Fine. May need to take a diversion. Roadworks. OK?'

'OK.'

Not a talker then, Claudia thought. That was good too. Give her time to process the events of the last hour. Her phone rang. She ignored it. He left a message. She knew it would be him without checking caller display. She watched the streetlights as they drove towards the edge of town. And she noticed the CCTV camera. That had been the start and end of the trouble: the camera in the corner of his office.

Claudia had fancied her boss from day one. It would be impossible to resist lusting after him. He was a charmer. Tall and slim. Dark hair and eyes, and an impeccable dresser. Oozed sexuality. Shame he'd turned out to be such a bastard, because Claudia and the director of marketing, Jon Gault, had been having fun. Until about 20 minutes ago, to be honest. And he'd certainly misjudged Claudia. She could take being fucked on his desk, she enjoyed it in fact. And she was happy knowing she wasn't the only one. She wasn't demanding exclusivity. With her record she wasn't in a position to. It was an open secret that Jon Gault had a wandering dick. But it was the being caught on camera she objected to. Not per se, of course. She and various exes had often enjoyed replaying their sexual antics on DVD. But that had been consensual. What she objected to was him filming it on the QT. She couldn't help but wonder if the contents of that little camera in the corner of the room, nominally there for security reasons, no doubt, would be uploaded to the internet. That some stranger in Canada or Brazil could be coming right now at the sight of her breasts being creamed over. And she had no idea where this left her in terms of employment either. Although, at times, she could take or leave her job. The politics and bitching got her down.

'You OK?'

Claudia caught the taxi driver's eye in the rearview mirror. Was it that obvious she was pissed off? If only the driver knew. She was unsatisfied too. She'd been on the verge of coming, rubbing his come into her breasts as his tongue flicked across her clit. She squeezed her thighs together, but the moment had passed. She pulled her jacket close round her body and shivered. She'd dressed quickly and carelessly, leaving as fast as she could. Her make-up was no doubt smudged, her hair awry, her shirt was buttoned, but only just. And usually she was such a careful dresser. She had enjoyed titillating Mr Gault in management meetings. Her skirts were tight. She wore stockings. And she would cross and uncross her legs as well as Sharon Stone, knowing he was itching to roll her skirt back, stroke her thighs, and delve into her sweet, wet, uncovered cunt. But instead he was forced to discuss their next big marketing campaign, with a hard-on he was struggling to keep hidden.

'Not really. Man trouble,' Claudia admitted, finally answering the driver's question.

'Men, eh? Who'd bother?' The driver held Claudia's gaze while they were waiting at traffic lights then she looked away. She was attractive. About Claudia's age. Short, choppy red hair.

'Not me, for a while, that's for sure,' Claudia replied. 'The male of the species can go fuck themselves as far as I'm concerned.'

'I'm with you on that one,' the driver replied.

They continued in silence for a few minutes. Claudia was beginning to relax. The heating was on, it was a cool night, and she was beginning to feel sleepy. She reached for her handbag, pulling it on her lap for comfort. Fuck. She had her handbag. But something was missing. Her laptop was back at the office. She couldn't afford to leave it there. She had emails to catch up on tonight, and she'd be for it if it got swiped.

Claudia leant forward and knocked on the glass.

'Sorry, you'll have to take me back. I've forgotten something.'

The driver was unfazed.

'No worries.'

She did a quick U-turn and drove Claudia back to the office, pulling into a parking space at the side of the building. Thank God he'd made her a key holder, Claudia thought. She knew no one would be around now. She and Jon had waited until the coast was clear. She grabbed the keys.

'Won't be a minute,' she told the driver.

'No worries, you want me to come in with you?'

Claudia shrugged. Not a bad suggestion. She'd never been in the building on her own. It couldn't hurt. That was the difference between women and men. Sisterhood. Not in the boardroom always, granted. But this woman was restoring her faith in humanity tonight.

'My name's Claudia, by the way.'

She couldn't explain what compelled her to tell this woman her name. There was something mesmerising about her. She was dressed casually. Dark jeans, white shirt. But then that suited her job. Her olive skin was smooth; she wore minimal but carefully applied make-up. Her dark eyes were outlined in kohl.

'I'm Anya.'

'Your name suits you.'

'Cheers.'

Claudia unlocked the door and Anya followed her into the building. They made straight for the lift, standing alongside one another, clothed arms almost touching as they waited for it to arrive. There was a definite frisson running between them, Claudia could sense it. Not fear, surely? Of being alone in the building. If so, why had she offered to accompany her?

'It's on the eighth floor,' Claudia said, to break the ice. 'You can wait here, if you like.'

'That's fine. I'll come up with you. I'm curious – never worked anywhere corporate. Can't see myself fitting in.'

Claudia looked at the woman more closely. Her nose was pierced with a tiny diamond. Her right ear had a row of tiny hoops in it. No doubt there were some tattoos and plenty of attitude hidden somewhere too. The company wanted ideas, but conformism. Not attitude. Anya was probably right. She wouldn't fit in. But Claudia doubted she would from now on either. Jon Gault would not take kindly to being spurned, and would resist accepting responsibility too.

'Doubt you would,' she replied. 'And doubt I will either, from tomorrow.'

'Rough day? I could tell you were troubled when you got into my cab.'

Anya rested her hand on Claudia's shoulder as the lift doors closed behind them. Claudia shivered. The other woman's touch was light but comforting.

'Yeah, got fucked by my boss today. Rather literally. In his office. It will be available for viewing on the internet later, I don't doubt. Without my consent.'

'What a bastard.' Anya's hand had crept up to Claudia's cheek. She stroked her fingers down and round her chin. This felt sweet. Then the lift doors opened. The two women stepped out into the dark corridor.

'It's just down here,' Claudia said, making her way to Jon's office. She knew it wouldn't be locked. He had a cavalier attitude, despite the camera in the corner of the room.

'Wow,' Anya gasped as Claudia slicked the lights on. One wall was just windows, giving a superb view over the city.

'Thank fuck it's still here. Let's go.' Claudia pulled her laptop case from under Jon's desk.

'Can we wait? A moment. I won't keep the clock running. I don't get to see the city from this vantage point.'

'If you like.' Claudia shrugged, joining Anya at the window. And then it happened. Anya turned to her, touched her face again, pushed her hair back. Her movements were

64

swift, familiar, tender, like those of a careful and gentle lover. Claudia closed her eyes. Anya placed her hands on Claudia's shoulders and turned her round. Then she kissed her. This wasn't entirely unexpected. But it felt bold. Her kiss was ardent. But still tender. Claudia felt a thrill of excitement rush through her. Anya pushed her lips apart with her tongue, explored her mouth. Her lips were full and warm. She and Jon didn't kiss. Not like this. Anya placed her hands on Claudia's face again, holding her firmly. The kiss lasted for an age. Then they pulled apart.

'I want to make you feel better,' Anya said. 'And I want you too.'

Claudia could see uncertainty on the other woman's face. She was taking a risk. Claudia had spoken of man trouble – suggested she was straight. But Anya must have sensed something. And she was right to have done so. Claudia had been attracted to this woman from the moment she'd got in the back of her cab.

'Over here.' Claudia took the lead now, indicating a leather sofa at right angles to the window. The two women fell onto it, kissing again, pressing their lips together. Anya had fallen on her back, Claudia on top, their limbs entangled. Claudia lifted herself slightly and began unbuttoning Anya's shirt. Braless, her breasts were small but firm and her dark nipples had tightened with desire. Claudia leant to take them in her mouth, one then the other, wetting them then blowing slightly. Anya groaned. Claudia was pleased. Do unto others was her motto. She took one nipple between her teeth, biting and pulling, circling it with her tongue, feeling her own desire mount as she did so. Then she reached down to the woman's jeans, unbuttoning them swiftly. She thrust her hand inside them; Anya was naked under her jeans. Claudia pushed her fingers between her lips, parting them gently, finding the other woman's clit. She pressed against the tiny nub for a moment, eliciting a moan. Anya was wet. Claudia's own cunt tightened as she felt Anya's desire. She pulled her fingers out, and licked Anya's juices from them.

'You taste good,' she whispered. Anya reached up and

began to unbutton Claudia's shirt, revealing a black lace bra. 'Pretty,' she added, reaching round the back and deftly unhooking it. Most men would have fumbled with it for a few moments at least. Claudia's full breasts fell out. She shook her shirt and bra off and discarded them. Like Anya, her nipples were tight with desire. Anya pulled Claudia down towards her, squeezing her breasts, taking first one then the other nipple between her teeth, flicking them with her tongue, twisting and biting, causing Claudia to writhe with pleasure. She wanted more of this woman. She wanted to fuck her, to please her, to satisfy her.

She lowered herself onto Anya. Her skin was warm and smooth. Her breathing was shallow with need. Anya's hands roved over Claudia's body. Claudia shivered as they reached the waistband of her skirt and flicked the button open, pushing the garment down over her hips. Turning to one side Claudia removed her skirt. Claudia saw Anya's eyes widen when she realised she was wearing stockings and no panties. Claudia rose to her on her knees, her legs either side of Anya's hips. Anya gazed at her. Their bodies contrasted with each other. Claudia was pale, full-bodied and shaven, while Anya was olive skinned and slim. Anya stroked her thigh, slowly walking her fingers up, touching her cunt lips with a feather-light touch. She parted them and found her clit.

'You're beautiful,' she whispered. Claudia rocked against Anya's fingers, her breasts aching with desire. Her cunt throbbed, and her juices ran down Anya's fingers.

'Inside me, please.'

'What's the rush,' Anya smiled. 'The clock's not ticking.' She pulled Claudia's hips forward, insinuating her fingers further between her thighs. Claudia was on fire. Her cunt tightened as Claudia pushed two, then three fingers inside her. She reached down to touch her clit, and Anya allowed her, her other hand resting on the small of Claudia's back, pulling her down rhythmically onto her fingers. As her orgasm threatened to overpower her Claudia sat back. She wasn't ready. Not yet. The two women made eye contact; they understood one another. Claudia tugged Anya's jeans over her hips, throwing them into the increasing pile of clothes. Then she sat back on her heels and looked.

Anya's legs were together, between Claudia's. Her hips were slender, almost boyish. She had a tattoo on her right side. "Sophia", it read, in rainbow colours. Claudia reached down and kissed it as she made her way to Anya's cunt with her tongue. Anya arched her back, raising her hips.

'The tattoo will last for ever, the woman left long ago,' she groaned.

'Life's a bitch,' Claudia murmured, getting to her feet. Anya looked surprised, disappointed. Claudia reached for her hand.

'Over here,' she whispered, leading her to Jon's desk. She swept the neatly stacked papers onto the floor then she switched on both the camera and laptop, checking to see the correct program was running. She pressed it on to "record". What would Jon and the world make of two women pleasuring each other? Claudia suspected it would turn him on – and that he would broadcast it. But he wouldn't be looking right now. He'd be on his way home. Now her pleasure, and Anya's, was paramount. She reached for two cushions from the sofa.

'Your turn,' Anya indicated that Claudia lie on the desk, so she did so. Some of the softness had gone from Anya's voice. She was assertive now, confident. No doubt she was more experienced with women than Claudia, who had always been curious, but so far had stopped at passionate kissing with a secretary at the Christmas party. She lay back, one cushion under her hips, the other under her head, feeling like a sacrificial victim, and that was fine. Anya circled the desk, running her fingers over Claudia's body, pinching her nipples, smoothing her skin. Claudia tried to lie still, but she could feel her body tighten and tense under the woman's touch. She felt elated, light-headed. And she was thirsting for more of this woman. She grasped her by the hand, pulling her closer. Anya, lithe and slim, lifted herself onto the desk and sat astride her, her cunt hovering over Claudia's, almost touching.

'I like stockings,' Anya whispered. 'A good old-fashioned touch, with a modern twist.' She stroked Claudia's shaven mound, parting her lips again with one hand. With the other she pulled back her suspender strap and allowed it to ping against Claudia's skin. The sweetest of stings, Claudia thought. She sat back and began licking Claudia's thighs, moving up, parting her lips, kissing her mound. Anya was an expert and Claudia quickly felt frantic with desire. What Anya was doing to her was all-consuming. Her hips bucked. Anya flattened her tongue and licked her clit. One master stroke almost pushed Claudia over the edge. Then she began flicking her tongue across it. Claudia writhed under her touch. Her knees were raised and she twisted and turned her hips, exposing herself to maximum pleasure. Anya twisted her nipples which were just within reach.

Claudia let out a groan. Anya's tongue was circling her clit now, exploring the area around it. She pulled one hand away from her breast and plunged three fingers deep into Claudia's cunt just as it began to spasm with orgasm. And then Claudia was gone. Her body pulsed with the rhythm of her pleasure. Her hips and legs trembled, and Anya kept on licking her clit, more gently now as the first intense waves began to subside. Claudia sighed as Anya pulled her face away, straddled Claudia again, cunt to cunt and began humping her. Her movements were frantic. She, too, seemed hot with desire. Claudia pulled Anya's face down to her, kissing her, insinuating her tongue between Anya's clenched teeth, tasting her own juices. She reached for Anya's clit, flicking it between her fingers.

'More,' Anya said, throwing her head back.

Claudia sat up and, deftly, the two women flipped over, understanding one another. Claudia was quick to press her face between Anya's open, inviting thighs. And Anya was equally quick to grab her hair and push her down. Anya's cunt was sweet, warm and wet. Luscious, in fact. Claudia began with frantic movements of her tongue, licking her clit, her lips, her inner thighs, her cunt itself. Her movements were urgent. She needed to please this woman. She took her clit in her mouth and sucked on it. Then she licked again, keeping a steady rhythm. She pushed fingers into Anya's cunt, feeling it tighten around them, and she thrust as she kicked. Anya cried out as her orgasm flooded through her. She bucked and heaved as Claudia satisfied her hunger. Once Claudia was quite certain Anya was satisfied, she lay down next to her, their legs entwined. They kissed – tiny feathery kisses. And they touched, exploring each other's bodies, Claudia's softness complementing Anya's firm edges. Already they understood each other. Claudia turned to the camera and gave it a smile and a wink.

'I could stay here all night, but there's fares out there waiting for a woman like me, so I'd better go. You coming?'

Claudia felt a twinge of envy at the thought of Anya with other women. They dressed quickly and in silence. Claudia turned the camera and laptop off and they went down together in the lift. Once Claudia had locked up they walked back out to the taxi, close together, their hands brushing. Claudia felt quite certain she would see Anya again.

'Where to?' Anya asked.

'Charles Street. Number 26.'

Anya nodded.

'May take a while. Roadworks. You OK now?'

Anya looked in her rearview mirror and smiled.

'I'm fine, look.' Claudia pulled her skirt to her hips, parted her legs and parted her lips with her fingers. She felt for her clit. It was tight and hard. She was wet from where their juices had mingled. When the taxi stopped at lights, she met Anya's gaze in the mirror. Their eyes locked. Now it was just the two of them. No cameras. Claudia wanted to leave Anya with the need to see her again and, from the look on the other woman's face, she thought she'd achieved that. Her cunt tightened round her fingers.

The cab pulled up to the curb. She was home. She paid Anya, tipping her generously and scribbling her name and number on a scrap of paper. No point in giving her a business card, because, as from tomorrow, she doubted she'd be employed there any more. But tonight had been worth it.

Roses and Figs
by Tabitha Rayne

Selena closed one eye and held out her arm, focusing on the end of her paintbrush. The woman lying naked before her on the silk-covered chaise longue was unlike any of her other clients. Usually when a woman came to her studio for a portrait, they would be nervous, birdlike, twittering with their hands trembling over buttons. Of course, Selena provided a screen and a robe to preserve their modesty but still most were self conscious and hesitant.

Usually Selena would discreetly leave to make coffee while they were changing, asking that they make themselves comfortable.

Rose had been different from the start. Before Selena could open the door fully, Rose had breezed past in her thick floor-length cashmere coat.

'Where do you want me?' she had declared and opened the coat to reveal a mass of naked flesh. Selena couldn't help staring as Rose let the single garment slide off her beautifully rounded shoulders and fall to the ground. She stepped out of the bundle of fabric in her heels and walked past the easel and over to the chaise longue. 'Will this do?' For her size, Rose was as elegant and graceful as a ballerina and sank softly into the cushions which seemed to catch her and lay her gently onto the couch.

Her pose was effortless and natural; she required no direction at all. Selena could only give a small shrug and whisper, 'That's perfect.' Rose's presence filled not only the sofa but the whole room and Selena found herself feeling quite

71

overwhelmed. She had never met anyone as self assured as this sensual, mighty woman.

The canvas seemed vast and empty and, for the first time ever, Selena thought she might have stage fright.

'Shall we begin?' She smiled at Rose and retreated behind the easel trying to compose herself. *Relax, relax, it's just the same as all the other times. All you need to do is paint.* Selena lifted her inked brush and held it out in front of her, repeating her usual mantra, *Paint what you see, paint what you see.*

But what she saw was magnificent. Rose had complete command over her body and had placed herself into a pose that showed off every curve and tone to perfection. Every angle, every joint, fingertip, toe had been very carefully and deliberately placed to display her Rubenesque figure beautifully.

Selena always had a bowl of fruit featured somewhere in her paintings, a throwback from art school where still life and life drawings were her favourite. She'd always thought the flesh of fruit and flesh of the human was a beautiful combination. It was now obvious that Rose felt the same; she had lifted out some grapes and figs and had them cradled in the crook of her arm spilling onto her breast and nipple. Selena took another breath and gazed at the scene. She looked up briefly from Rose's chest and caught her eye. Rose gave her a cheeky smile and squeezed her elbow in a little to push the fruit and breast out even more. Selena realised her arm was still in the same outstretched position and getting a cramp. She took the measurement and went to make the first mark on her page. Her brush hovered and her mind seemed to stop. All she could do was stare at the pure white of the canvas. *Just paint!*

When Selena had finally composed herself, she took one quick glimpse then swept her brush across the page. Phew! The first was always the most awkward, the blank canvas the most difficult part to navigate. She looked at the line. Good. It was good. Strong and compelling. Just like her subject. Selena was desperately trying not to admit to herself that she was becoming aroused by this incredibly sensual woman lying in front of her. She knew she was hiding behind the easel, taking far too long over the stroke – she was a professional for God's sake – the sketching should be done by now!

She could hear a soft moist noise coming from the sofa and she carefully looked round. Rose had a very ripe fig pressed up against her lips and the juice was sliding down her chin and onto her chest. Rose watched Selena watching the succulent flesh slip slowly towards her nipple. Selena was transfixed. The juice and pips made it to Rose's nipple and her chest rose as the dark pink skin tightened and puckered. *Oh my God*, thought Selena as she looked up at Rose's hooded eyes, *she's trying to turn me on!* She retreated once more and swiped at the canvas with her brush, furiously trying to shake off her lustful feelings. It was no good. She peeked again only to see that Rose had shifted her buttocks slightly and let her leg drop open revealing a mist of hair between her thighs. She was greedily sucking the last of the fig from its skin and tossed it on the floor. She reached for another and eased herself further down the sofa, arching her back and stretching out like a cat.

'I'm sorry,' muttered Selena, 'but you can't keep moving about. I've already marked your previous pose.'

'Oh, I'm sorry, honey.' Rose's voice was thick and purring. She sighed and shifted her body saying, 'Was I like this?'

Rose was facing Selena full on with her legs eased apart. The fruit had fallen from her chest and had come to rest between her thighs. Rose plucked out a grape and popped it in her mouth staring at Selena all the while. Selena felt herself begin to burn.

'No. Maybe I should come and re-position you.'

'If you think it will help.' Rose smiled, letting her head fall back slightly as Selena approached.

Selena's hands were trembling as she patted the headrest of the chaise longue. 'You're head was up here.'

'Was it?' Rose held out her arm for Selena to help ease her back up. Selena locked elbows and shivered as she felt the strength in the muscles beneath the soft undulating flesh. Rose still had the fig in her hand and it brushed past Selena's shirt as she released her grip. Selena felt the damp material cling to her breast and busied herself arranging Rose's hair.

'Oops, sorry,' Rose said, allowing herself to be positioned. 'I seem to have got fig all over you.'

'Don't worry about it.' Selena continued to primp and manoeuvre, but as she did so she felt Rose's hand cup her left breast. Selena needed to make a decision. She felt her nipples stiffen as Rose lightly brushed one with her thumb. *Oh my God.* Selena was frozen to the spot. Nothing like this had ever happened to her and she had no idea what to do. She focused on Rose's hair which she had fanned out onto the headrest and pretended not to notice the heat that was spreading through her pelvis.

Selena was still staring at Rose's hair when she felt her nipple dampen; she chanced a quick look and saw that Rose was pressing half a fig onto her breast. Selena let herself relax slightly as the fruit was massaged and squeezed onto her through her shirt. Her legs wobbled and she adjusted her feet to keep her balance. Rose kept rubbing and the fig was warming up, juice trickling down Selena's chest and stomach to her waistband.

'Do you know, honey,' Rose spoke softly, 'in some cultures, men practise cunnilingus on figs.'

'Really?' Selena could only squeak her response as Rose kept teasing and massaging her, more quickly now, and rough.

'Have you ever tried?'

'Figs?' Selena was really off balance now and had to take more weight with her arms on the chaise longue. Her breasts were now hovering close to Rose's face and she could smell the sticky fruit on her breath.

'No, honey, not figs.' Rose slowly leant in and removed the fig from Selena's breast and replaced it with her mouth. Selena gasped as warmth engulfed her while Rose sucked and tongued her nipple through her cotton shirt. She let herself give in to the soft, glorious feeling of having another woman suckle her. She looked down and watched Rose's lips pucker and release while she gently groaned.

Rose's groans were getting more intense and Selena could see her body bucking and heaving beneath her. She looked lower to see that Rose's hand had rolled down between her

74

thighs, leaving a trail of sticky fig juice all the way. She could see her rubbing herself between her thighs with the fruit, round and round, all the while sucking at Selena's breast.

Selena made her decision. She wanted more. She pushed herself to her feet and undid the buttons of her shirt and pulled it off.

'Atta girl,' purred Rose and pulled Selena back towards her with her free hand. Selena's naked breast swayed straight back into Rose's mouth and she engulfed it in hot wet saliva. Selena let out a yelp and fell to her knees as Rose nibbled her with teeth, but it felt so good. Selena's knickers grow hot and moist and clamped her thighs together to try and get some relief. She ground her pelvis into the side of the chaise longue.

Rose reached up and took Selena's hand in her fig-covered fingers. She held it tight and slowly pulled it down towards her crotch. Selena hesitated; she had never felt another woman before.

'It's all right, honey,' Rose assured her, 'you'll be good.' Selena relaxed a little and let Rose take control once more. She clasped her fig-stained fingers and pushed them onto her downy mound. Rose brought her knees up and parted them. Selena could feel the slippery skin on her fingertips and Rose held her more tightly, guiding her down between her lips. Round and round over the hard bud went her hands. Rose was moving herself in time with the motion and Selena could feel her heat and wetness intensify. Rose's hand gripped hers tightly and Selena gasped as Rose pushed her fingers deep inside her. Selena managed to release her thumb and began to tentatively rub Rose's clitoris round and round like before. Rose groaned and took her hands from around Selena's. Selena massaged Rose more quickly with her fingers buried deep inside and her thumb teasing her bud. The walls of Rose's pussy began to buck and spasm around their fingers and Selena felt a gush of warmth engulf her hand and trickle down her wrist. She left her hand for a few more moments covered in fig and love juice while Rose twitched and contracted back to calm.

Selena was panting and confused – *Had that really just*

happened? She looked up at Rose who returned her gaze with a flushed radiant smile.

Selena stood up to go back to her painting but Rose reached out and pulled her by the hem of her skirt. She sat upright and ran her hands up Selena's thighs, pushing her skirt over her hips.

'Your turn, honey.' She grinned and hooked her index finger into Selena's panties, pulling them to the side. Selena shivered as she watched the thick mass of Rose's hair lean in towards her. *I am an artist*, she said to herself, *I need to know about these things*. There was no going back now and Selena slid her feet further apart. She could feel Rose's nose nuzzling in to her, breathing in her fragrance. Selena felt a jolt of electricity as Rose's tongue darted on to her clitoris. It was so quick, so strange, so exciting. She felt a rush of want in her pelvis and rocked herself towards Rose's face. She noticed one of Rose's hands leave her thigh and watched as it slid along to the discarded fruit from earlier. Selena watched Rose grapple for a grape and took it back towards her pussy. Rose looked up to Selena and put the grape to her lips, and seductively bit it in half. She took one of the halves and gently opened Selena's vulva and rubbed her with the cool fruit.

The hairs on Selena's arms and neck stood up as Rose sucked the grape from her bud and replaced it with her tongue. She couldn't help but grasp handfuls of the voluptuous woman's hair and draw her into her. Rose's tongue flicked and danced on her clit but Selena needed more. The walls of her pussy ached to grip something, anything! As if reading her thoughts, Rose reached out for another grape and held it between her fingertips. Slowly, while still licking her clitoris, she ran the grape around the entrance to Selena's pussy. Round and round she teased; Selena thought she would scream until, at last, she eased the grape into the yearning cave of Selena. She could feel herself twitching around the fruit and had never felt so turned on. Rose, still holding it, pushed it in and out in rhythm with her licking.

'Harder!' shrieked Selena before she could stop herself and raked her nails into Rose's scalp. Rose didn't need any more encouragement and quickened her pace and strength, sliding her tongue and fingers into every part of Selena. With one last hard thrust, Selena's body went rigid while she shuddered to a climax on top of Rose. She felt her energy drain from her and slumped to her knees in front of Rose. Rose slid her fingers from Selena and popped the grape into her mouth, savouring its slippery warmth.

'Mmm,' she said, easing herself back onto the chaise longue. 'Now, where were we?'

Selena, exhausted, pulled herself up with her elbows beside Rose. 'I was re-positioning you,' she panted and flopped her head onto Rose, laughing.

Rose nudged Selena to her feet and started to rearrange herself. Selena picked up her shirt and went behind her easel to dress. She suddenly felt very naked with her skirt hitched up and no top on. When she had composed herself and picked up her paintbrush ready to continue, she peered around her easel. To her astonishment, Rose was in the exact place as before, grapes in the crook of her arm and a fig poised at her lips.

Selena trembled with post-orgasm dizziness. The palette felt heavy in her arms and she struggled to regain her focus. She gave herself a shake. *I am a professional*, she told herself and took a deep breath. Rose lay on the chaise longue as calm and as self composed as ever. Selena swept the brush across the canvas.

As Selena added the final strokes, Rose stretched and got to her feet, scattering fruit over the floor. She pulled on her cashmere coat and turned to look at the painting.

'Not bad, honey,' she said. 'Not bad at all.' And with that, she breezed past Selena once more and out through the front door.

Later, when the paints and brushes were cleaned and the room had been put to rights, Selena's hand hovered over the fruit bowl. She couldn't resist picking up a soft ripe fig and putting it to her lips …

When I Am Niki
by Amanda Stiles

When I arrived she was wearing thigh-highs and high-heels and thick black eyeliner. It was sort of our ritual. Looking at her reminded me of the sex. Sex we'd shared on other days, the sex we were *going* to have that day. My heart pounded and an electric feeling jolted my body. She stood and waited, arms folded across her bare breasts, while I undressed and then redressed. I sat down on the edge of the bed, dressed much the same as she, in black thigh-highs and black patent leather stilettos. I *adored* the high-heels. They made me feel sexy and I liked the way my legs and ass looked with them on. She knelt before me with the pony-tail plug laid out across her palms. It was her favourite, and mine also. I loved to watch the tail as it hung, swaying from her backside. I took the buttplug from her and held it upright between my legs. Obediently, she fellated my faux-erection for a moment, and then picked up the bottle of sex-goo that lay on the floor by her knee. She lubed the length of the plug with one hand as she looked up at me, silently, with pleading brown eyes.

Melissa – I called her *Mel* – stood and turned and bent at the waist. She pulled her dizzying ass cheeks apart before me. The bright red fingernails furrowed and creased her cheeks, and the pony tail rustled as I touched the tip to her asshole. The plug was six inches long and a little bigger around than a quarter at its widest. Mel sucked in a breath and pulled her ass cheeks wider. The greased dildo started inward and Mel sucked in another deep breath. I pushed until the apex of the plug stretched her asshole to a thin, tight membrane and then disappeared. My palm landed a sharp, congratulatory smack against her ass.

Mel knew the deal. After the plug was in place, I lay back on the bed and lit a cigarette. I spread my legs wide apart, slowly, in spite of the agonising anticipation. I looked down past the features of my body, and Mel looked up at me as she eased between my thighs. My pussy *burned*. Her tongue touched, soft and warm, against my clitoris, and then inside me. I blew a billowy cloud of cigarette smoke at her face. She licked several times against my clit and then sucked it between her lips. I pulled and twisted my nipples erect. My hips lifted and lowered evenly, helpless to be still. I flicked cigarette ash at her face – she liked that – as she sucked my horny, *aching* pussy.

I finished the cig and dropped it into the glass on the nightstand, then reached down as I raised my legs up over my head and pulled *my* cheeks apart. Again, Mel knew the deal and she submitted. Her tongue swirled my asshole and then pushed *in*. I pulled her face against my cheeks until her tongue fucked in as deep as it would go. God, I loved her.

I lowered my legs and spread them wide and locked straight. Mel's lips again found my clit. Her tongue flicked at the tip, and then her cool, slender fingers entered my openness. I moaned. Mel sucked my clit and fucked my pussy, until my abdomen and ass cheeks clenched and my hips bucked uncontrollably. The pleasure waned gradually as my body relaxed.

She immediately rolled off the bed and retrieved the strap-on. We called it "Frank". The dildo was considerably larger than the typical penis, much larger than Mr Jeffrey's. Mel said 'Penises are for making love, but *dildos* are for *fucking*'. She manoeuvred the strap-on in place on my body and cinched it comfortably tight. I uttered pretend-groans of encouragement as she sucked the head and stroked the shaft of my fake cock.

I stood at the foot of the bed and lathered the dildo with the lube. I inhaled deeply, savouring the mingled aromas of sex lubricant and pussy. Mel lay face down on the bed with her legs apart, her cunt-hole swollen and open and ready. I flipped the pony tail up onto her lower back, knelt between Mel's legs and slapped Frank's bulbous head against her twat. She held her breath. I eased the mammoth prick into her pussy, almost halfway, and then laid myself down atop her warm soft body. I grasped her wrists with my hands above her head to keep her from masturbating. We *both* enjoyed those frantic moments of orgasm denial when pleasure has gone too far and release is teased near then cruelly shooed away.

I fucked slow and deep and Mel's hips lifted in time with my thrusts. It wasn't long before I had to strain to keep her hands under control. Mel's rapid breaths and squirming body belied her nymphomaniac desires. The harder, the deeper the thrusts, the louder the panting, the more fervent the squirming. I *loved* that I was making her feel so good.

Twice in quick succession Mel's hand wrested free, and I fought to regain control of her. I reared up and back, and took a handful of her hair in my hand and pulled, hard, until Mel was up on her hands and knees. I jerked the plug from her asshole, and she chirped in protest. I swatted her ass hard with the tail and tossed the buttplug aside.

I touched Frank's head to Mel's butthole. She sucked in yet another deep breath and held it, then pushed her hips backward and practically impaled herself on the massive, latex fuck-stick strapped around my hips. She exhaled sharply through her tightly clenched teeth. I wrapped my hands around her waist and fucked her as she fucked me back. This time I allowed Mel to masturbate at will. I twiddled my nipples with my thumb-tips as I watched Mel finger pleasure into her pussy with obsessive purposefulness. I loved the way her ass spasmed and flexed when she came, and I let her come twice. I wished I could come inside her.

By noon we were pretty loaded on screwdrivers of mostly vodka and the thin taste of orange juice. We spent the afternoon fucking, at times like lovers, at times like animals. Mel liked the collar and leash and the crop. I led her around on her hands and knees on the living room carpet and made her lick my pussy and my asshole while I stood over her. I striped her ass red with the crop while she fingered herself. We fucked in the shower, on the deck in the hot sun, and we took turns eating each other's pussies on the stairs.

The Jeffreys, Paul and Melissa, hired me two years ago. I was 24 then. Mel is five years older than me; Paul is six years older than she. He is a fairly accomplished architect, works on a number of municipal projects in Midwestern cities, and travels quite a lot. I serve as Mel's assistant. I help her with life's tedium and coordinate her appointments. Nothing too glorious. Mostly nail and hair and spa appointments. I accompany her on shopping trips and do all the cooking and buy the groceries. Most of the housekeeping is taken care of by the maid service. Sometimes Mel keeps me pretty busy. Sometimes we just goof off. Sometimes we just *fuck*. I practically live at the Jeffreys' during the week, but the weekends are mine. I keep a small apartment on the other side of town, which they pay for.

Mel and I began to "explore" our friendship about a month after I started working for her. Mel said she'd never thought about fucking a woman before. We were lounging and drinking on the back deck. After a couple of hours in the hot sun, she suggested we "cool off" in the shower. She made the first move by offering to wash my tits. Her eyes flashed with a mad lust, which surprised me at first. 'I'd love it,' I told her, and she lathered my breasts. Then we kissed in the warming stream of the shower. The rest of the day was a blur of excitement, feelings almost like a crush. I have no words for the intensity of the pleasures and the orgasms.

It was *hardly* my first taste of pussy, but Mel has helped me understand how much I appreciate being with a woman. Not that I've given up on men. No way. I still love a stiff thick cock, and being with a woman a lot can really make you miss a man. You expect a woman to be soft, gentle, graceful, beautiful, fragrant. Being with a guy, you expect him to be strong and rough and coarse. It's part of the fun. But, when a guy is gentle and patient and humble, the contrast kind of blows me away. So I still see guys. On *my* time.

Mel likes being dominated, and I found that the kink was a fucking turn-on for me. At first I thought it was weird that I worked for Mel, yet *I* was the one being dominant. If someone had told me beforehand that I was going to be having a kinky affair with my boss, I would have pictured it the other way around. Now it just seems natural. Mel likes me to stuff panties into her mouth and slap her face and call her 'whore' and 'slut'. Sometimes I write such words on her body in red lipstick, and penetrate her ass and pussy and mouth with various toys and take pictures. We sit at her computer desk and look at the pictures, huddled together, masturbating ourselves and each other, chain-smoking and drinking ourselves stupid. I like Mel a lot. Actually, I love her. I would do anything for her. I just about have …

Six months after I started working for the Jeffreys, Mel unveiled a devious plan. Paul was in town. In the late afternoon, she pretended to head off for yoga. I pretended I had work to finish up. Mel hid in the master closet with the door open a crack. I flirted a little with Mr Jeffrey until we were up in the bedroom. I sucked him off on my knees at the foot of the bed. He came in my mouth and I swallowed his come; he seemed to appreciate that. I heard the muffled sounds of Mel masturbating, which kind of scared me, so I moaned loudly to cover it up. Afterwards, I had to get Mr Jeffrey back downstairs so Mel could sneak out and then come back in. I implored him to show me how to make martinis in the kitchen. Mel walked in with her yoga mat rolled up and tucked under her arm. Mr Jeffrey acted guilty as sin. It was kind of funny. I got a raise a couple of weeks later, and I still wonder if the raise was Mel's idea, or Paul's; I never asked. Mel gloated that Paul never breathed a word about the blowjob. A couple of other times I actually fucked him in their bed in similar, contrived situations. Mel said, 'I love the taste of your pussy on Paul's cock.' And we laughed at the thought of Mel walking in at the "right moment". Paul would have shit himself. He's a really good guy. Very sweet and gentle. I think that is why Mel likes me to dominate her. I'm not so sure he could pull it off – being that "cruel-to-be-kind" sort of lover.

I asked Mel if she'd ever want to do a three-way with Paul. She said, 'God, no, I wouldn't!' and then, 'I hate to admit this, but I don't want Paul to ever know of this part of me!' I shrugged. Whatever. I guess Mel liked having her secrets. I think I understood. The secrets are their own wicked pleasure.

Once, Mel took me to California with her for a week. We shopped and dined on Rodeo Drive. In a week's time we fucked in half the restrooms and dressing rooms along that little stretch of shopping heaven. We laughed pretty hard about that. Two women can go in *anywhere* together, but if a man and a woman went into the restroom at the same time, someone would be having a shit-fit for sure. She bought me some really nice things. She liked flirting with the guys. It was all teasing. She liked the way they looked at us, and said it was a turn-on. She'd flirt, lead them on then leave them flat. It was funny and it was sad too. For the guys, I mean.

The last night in LA, Mel had me parade her around a few of the nightclubs with a black collar and chrome-link leash. She wore a low-cut, short and super-tight black dress and did her make-up like the whore of all whores. I told her to put in a smallish buttplug before we went out. She took the plug out in the cab on the way home and sucked on it until the cabbie looked at her through the rearview mirror. His voice shook when he spoke after that. She was – I should say *we* – were quite a spectacle. It was fun getting so much attention and it made us both horny as fuck. We took care of that back at the hotel.

The sun was almost setting. I woke up on the sofa with both my arms around Mel, and I felt hungry. I patted Mel on her ass. When she woke, she lifted her head off my shoulder and blew late-day, boozy, morning-breath in my face. I put on a pot of coffee and then we sat, naked and cross-legged on the couch and smoked cigarettes and drank coffee, until we were both alive enough to think about getting dinner.

We got showered and dressed and put on fresh make-up. I drove Mel downtown in her Audi. We ate filet mignon and asparagus with béarnaise sauce, and drank a private reserve cabernet sauvignon. A good hour passed while we window-shopped, hand in hand. We ended up at a club off 72nd, and danced a ton, mostly with each other. By midnight we were off our asses again. I hate driving drunk. I smoked cigarette after cigarette as we carefully made our way home.

Mel toppled onto the bed and I kicked off my shoes and rolled onto the bed next to her. We kissed a soft and sensual and long lady-kiss. 'You want to fuck?' Mel whispered. 'Yes.' I whispered back.

I sucked Mel's lower lip into my mouth and bit down gently, coaxing the hem of her dress up the curve of her beautiful ass. With just the tips of my nails I traced lightly up and down her thigh and ass cheek. Mel draped her leg across mine and raised it until her bent knee was above my waist. I touched my fingertips to the cleft between her cheeks, barely, with the lightest of touches. The kind that gives you the chills. Mel was already breathing hotly. I circled a fingertip in a wide arc around her pussy then commenced to explore its slick, dripping folds.

Touching Mel's wet pussy made mine tingle and swell and I wanted to come terribly. I kissed my tongue deep into her mouth as I pushed my fingers into her begging twat. She moaned and I could feel myself heaving for breath. I felt her fingers reach into the top of my dress and she found my nipples. My body ignited to her touch.

I raised a hip and tugged at my dress. Mel helped me pull it up, over my head until it was off and I tossed it at the foot of the bed. I helped her out of hers and then pushed her legs apart roughly, hooked my arms around her thighs and sucked her abundant pussy into my mouth. Mel's cunt poured and I swallowed all I could. I hooked the middle and index fingers of my right hand into my pussy and tugged rhythmically. My whole body burned.

I straddled Mel's face and lowered my hips, and again sucked her entire pussy into my mouth. I love the way her lips and clit swell, firm and full and tight, when she is alight with the kind of desire that turns into *need*. I twisted her nipples and she fingerfucked my asshole and sucked and nibbled at my aching kitty. The sensations overwhelmed – every nerve in my body raged. I humped my hips down against Mel's face as she serviced my clit. Pulsing tremors of pre-orgasm ripped through me and, as I bit down on Mel's innermost thigh, I came, hips pumping, with not a shred of dignity – beyond any glimmer of self-control.

Mel and I have always fed on each other's sexual energies. Mel growled as I came and spread her legs wide and out straight like a porn actress. She reached down and fucked the first two fingers of each her hands into her own pussy, pulled it wide open, and drove the fingers inward. I took her clit in my mouth and she four-finger fucked herself while I sucked. She endured a protracted, gut-crunching climax with much swearing. I knew from *that* orgasm that we were only just getting started.

Mel went slack beneath me and then slapped my ass several times. I rolled off her and turned and looked at her sweating face. 'Fuck me ... please ... nasty ... with Jerry.' Jerry was *way* longer than Frank, just not as thick.

With Jerry's long, shining, gently-curved blackness strapped to my body, I pulled Mel's hair as I fucked her face. She gagged as she tried to throat the dildo. I wondered if she ever ate Paul's cock with the same eager enthusiasm. Tears melted her eyeliner and dribbled dark streaks down her face. I rolled her onto her back and pinned her knees to her armpits with my palms, fucking Jerry into her pussy, just like a man would, with my torso elevated and arms straight. I liked how my tits swung as I fucked in and mashed my clit against her clit as she lifted her hips and hoarsely begged me to fuck her '*harder*'.

I fucked and fucked, until my ass cheeks and legs began to burn with the effort. Being the "man" is a lot of work. Mel came, practically screaming. I wondered if I had a real cock, if it would be difficult to keep an erection with the woman making so much noise. A *real* man wouldn't have a problem with it, I'm sure.

Mel's orgasm made me extremely edgy. I knew what she was going to get next, but I needed some first. *A girl's got to do what a girl's got to do ...* I got up off the bed and found the slender pink vibrator. I lubed it and eased it into my ass and twisted it on, and then loosened Jerry's straps. I stood on my knees between Mel's legs as I fucked the vibrator up my asshole with one hand, and rubbed my pussy, crazy-fast, with the other. Mel looked at me, with her legs up and back, and pulled her asshole open for me as she watched me "jill off". The release came quick, and it helped me get back on track. I pulled the vibrator out and re-tightened Jerry's straps as I caught my breath.

If I was patient and slow and gentle, I knew I could get most of Jerry up Mel's ass. We'd done it before. It made my pussy tingle to imagine all of Jerry there. Mel closed her eyes as I pushed. I paid very careful attention to her expressions. The first six inches moved in easily then I pushed more slowly. Mel grimaced and I paused. I touched my thumb to her clit and the corner of her mouth bent in a smile. I raised the angle and pushed then lowered the angle and made another gentle, easy push.

One day we'd measured a good ten inches of anal penetration with Jerry up Mel's ass. She was pretty proud of it. She said it hurt a little, but the pain turned her on. I told her she should be doing porn. She joked that she would if I would. I admit that I'd do it if Mel did – the thought of fucking Mel in front of a camera turns me on – but I honestly don't have *any* idea how to get into porn.

There was enough of Jerry still out of Mel that I could wrap four fingers around the last of the shaft. That meant maybe three inches. Jerry was a full 12 inches. I pushed again. Mel grimaced then croaked, 'That's plenty, babe.'

'No fucking way,' I shot back, sternly.

'N–o–o–o …' Mel moaned. Her lip quivered as she tried to force a smile.

The vibrator buzzed alive. I teased Mel's clit until her pussy splayed open, and the walls of her vagina pouted out between the lips. Repeatedly I denied her the orgasm, as I adjusted Jerry's angle and nudged. A little further, then a bit more. I looked down. I slapped at Mel's hands when she tried to touch herself, and I raised and lowered Jerry's angle again and *pushed*. Mel's ass cheeks touched against the top of my thighs, and I fucked in hard till my body mashed against hers.

'Ohhh … Gawwwd …' followed by a low, otherworldly groan.

I liked it when Mel was so desperate for release she actually sobbed. Sometimes those sobs put a lump in my throat. To hasten the sobbing, and to heighten my own hunger, I slapped her tits and twisted her nipples and slapped her across the face.

Tears welled in Mel's eyes. 'Please … pleeeease …' she begged. I slapped her face again, harder. A plaintive sob. I twisted her right nipple viciously then touched the vibrator to her clit and raised it away when she lifted her hips. A mournful sob followed by gagging and she wept openly. I rotated my hips to make room, turned the palm up on my left hand, and slipped three fingers into her swollen twat then returned the vibrator to her clit. Her hips lifted, instantly, forcefully. The weeping became a tortured howl. I fucked the fingers in and out as fast as I could. Mel's entire body cramped tight – I could see the muscles of her arms and legs and chest and stomach flexed and straining, and the sinews in her neck stood out. Mel's eyes squeezed shut and then opened frightfully wide. She came, shaking violently and *shish-shish-shish*-ing for breath through her clenched teeth.

She flung her body against the bed as the orgasm finally subsided. Mel groaned 'Ohh! Fuck!'

'I'm coming!' I returned. I eased the dildo out of her ass and scrambled up her body, stroking the shaft as I moved. Mel gobbled the head, ravenously. I jacked Frank's length mimicking frantic urgency. 'Ohh … fuck, babe. Suck my cock. Oh, God! Ohh … fuck! Suck my cock! Swallow my come! Ohhh!' I flexed my body hard as if I were coming. Mel sucked the head and then kissed it as the "orgasm" subsided.

I loosened the straps on Jerry, pulled it out of my way, and lowered my pussy to Mel's face. Her lips found my clit and the *real* magic started. I scrubbed my pussy against her face as I fingered my own asshole. The orgasm was brutal. Almost painful. So violent, so consuming, it gave me stomach ache. My asshole and pussy tingled fiercely, even after the orgasm was gone.

I collapsed against the headboard. I wanted a cigarette and a drink. Mel's hands coursed gingerly up and down my body. 'I love you, Niki,' Mel whispered. My given name is Celia. I am Niki when we fuck. 'I … love … you … too … bitch,' I huffed in reply, still gasping for breath.

An Evening Stroll
by Z Ferguson

My name is Pam and my roommate's name is Dora. I call her Dora the Explorer, because of her adult likeness to the animated child star. She sports a raven black page boy and large deep brown eyes that I can't lie to, even if I wanted. She's six foot to my five-four, a tower to my tiny blonde carriage.

In college, Dora used to do field events in track and play field hockey. That should give you her body type: athletic with broad shoulders, muscled calves and thighs. Even at 30 (Dora won't admit to any number higher), her body is taut and exciting. Large breasts that barely shimmy when she's topless on the beach. I get wet waiting to apply her sunscreen.

She has this muscle on her thigh that rubs my clit just right when I slide astride her leg. She calls me her love slug because of the trail I leave on her leg when I come.

She calls me Pammy whenever she has thought of an "adventure" we can share, saying my name in a low register, conspiratorial, like it's something no one else should know about.

'Pammy, let's go to Upper Kinnear Park and watch the sun set over the city.'

'OK.'

Already I feel my pussy tick like a bomb set to go off. My head is swimming trying to think of what Dora will want me to do.

Last week, she pleasured me with a zucchini in the women's restroom at the local grocers. We bought it, the clerk

91

put it in the bag, and when we went to the restroom, Dora turned me facing the sink, lifted my skirt (Dora insists on my wearing skirts, as she wants complete and total access to me at all times), and rammed that veggie into my pleasure hole, while I stood facing the mirror. She pulled my panties down and really gave it to me, as I clutched the basin. I was so scared someone might come in, but so aroused thinking someone might come in, that Mr Zuke was coated in my juices and made for a wonderful ride. I came hard and shook the sink, my legs open, on my tiptoes in my tennie runners.

That night, after zucchini bread for dessert, we bathed each other and I ran my soapy hands all over Dora's body and between her legs. Dora didn't want me to use a towel or a luffa, just my hands and fingers in all the right places. She came like a volcano, in hefty body shakes, and with a crimson face, as she stood in the tub. I could barely keep my lips on her pussy as she shuddered and clutched my head for balance. In bed, I ran my pussy along that wonderful muscle on her thigh and rejoiced into her hard stomach.

Then there was the time she had me pose naked for her artist friends. I was on a small pedestal, and they were allowed not only to make sketches and render studies but to touch and fondle me however they wanted. One guy had me spread my legs then he ran his long slithery tongue between the cheeks of my ass to my pussy to the small of my back. Another woman played a black leather gloved hand on my nipples until I needed to come so bad Dora had to take me into the bedroom and do me, so I could stand still for the rest of the evening. When I emerged and took my place on the pedestal, the members took turns licking and sucking me. An older man took to the pedestal and pulled out his large gnarled cock. I looked at Dora for permission. She nodded and took a drag from her cigarette, as I lowered myself onto his dick, and fucked him until the delight left his eyes and entered my body.

My most memorable adventure was when we went on a dinner date and she kept me naked all evening. She booked a reservation at the Sorrento Hotel. (Dora knew a waiter who held a private booth for us.)

The looks we got as I strolled in on my stiletto heels and Dora in her little black dress. We sat, me naked and she clothed. She popped the champagne and I popped the waiter (with Dora's permission). Champagne and waiter come caught each other in mid-flight. It was a wonderful meal and I climaxed several times in the car coming home, Dora allowing me to pleasure myself. I slept well that night.

Dora checks me over. She lifts my dress to see if I'm wearing panties. I am. Her favourites – the white cotton mid-waists. She runs her hand over them in approval. She stands and looks at me while holding my shoulders.

'Tonight's adventure is special, but first we have to watch the sun set over the city. It's lovely. Just like you, Pammy.'

I blush.

Dora is going retro tonight. Tight jeans, a white shirt tied at the waist and no bra. A small black clutch purse in her hand. She draws many eyes as we walk along Kinnear Park on Upper Queen Anne. I'm in a pink flowered party dress, with black ballet slippers. I'm wearing a wide-brim hat because of the sun. Dora is very protective of my skin.

We find a park bench and sit. There are other people up there, families, teen lovers, kids, all talking and sitting around on benches or brought-out chairs waiting for the sunset. The air is still and I hear gentle laughter and conversation all around me. Everyone is bathed in the changing light. Dora holds my hand. 'I'm very excited about tonight,' she says, lighting a cigarette, 'you'll love it, Pammy.'

I know I will.

The sun cast a warm pink hue over the city skyline. There were oohs and aahs, as it disappeared, and the last of its rays brought the colour down like a curtain in a final production. The evening ascended, and parents prepared their kids for bed, teens and their dates vanished further into the park. Streetlights and warm golden houselights eased on as night caressed the city. The skyline sparkled in city lights. Dora raised her hand and motioned it downward. That meant panties off.

I shuddered and looked around.

'Focus on me, Pammy, not them. This is *our* adventure.'

I stood and raised my party dress, my eyes on Dora, then rolled the panties off my hips and down to my bare ankles, and sat with them bunched at my feet, rolled like cotton leg-irons. My ass was chilly-thrilly on the wooden bench. Several couples walked by and looked at me. I stared straight ahead.

One guy stopped. He was Northwest handsome in that semi-scruffy way, with light brown shaggy hair and piercing eyes. Large hands. His shorts were pronounced with cock as he stared at me. Our eyes locked. I felt the panty anklets on my shins. Dora watched him.

'We're fine, sir,' she said. He continued on as Dora watched him. Dora's tone of voice speaks no nonsense and people seem to understand. It's exciting to see her wave them away with her verbiage.

Dora raises her hand, turns her palm up. I step out of the panties and hand them to her. She feels them with both hands then stuffs them into her clutch and snaps it shut. The snap is loud and my vag drips whenever I hear it. I know my little dew dish will remain bare for the rest of the evening. She stands and heads to the restroom. I watch her confident walk and swaying bottom as she steps down to the bathrooms in the park. She didn't call for me so I stayed. People walked by and smiled. I smiled back and crossed my legs, bobbing the top leg in tight nods. I used this to get myself off, though I was already very close, from feeling my bare butt on the bench, nodded greetings at couples and singles, young and old, as they walked by.

Knowing I'm a fabric's breath away from showing my puss has stripped my resolve. Like flicks on a stubborn lighter, each flick of my bare leg brings me closer to igniting in a very public ecstasy. My leg quickens, pulse races. I spread my toes to retain my shoe and look to the sky, stretching my throat and feeling the come radiate throughout my body. My hands grip my thighs then slide to grip the slats in the bench. I fight the urge to throw my legs open and finger myself. My breasts jump and quiver; I eek. A gay couple smile as they stroll by.

94

'You go, girl,' one of them whispers.

I glance at the restrooms and Dora is talking to the young man that earlier she dismissed. I scrunch my nose in curiosity as they both look my way. Dora leaves him, approaching me. An adventure is in the making. In vivid throbs, my pussy agrees. Dora sits beside me, sniffs the air and smiles. Her nostrils emit a knowing flare.

'Naughty girl … Well, I guess we better head back home. I think you need to go to the restroom before we leave though. It's a bit of a walk back.'

We stand and Dora grabs my hand. We stroll to the rest area, two restrooms in an ivy-covered concrete saltbox. We enter the men's side. I look at Dora.

'The women's side is broken, Pammy. Sit. I'll watch out front.'

I nod, lifting my skirt. Dora watches until my skirt is completely up and my pussy is exposed. I sit and I take a touch of my pussy lips while she watches and smiles. 'You horny little bitch,' she says in a smirk, 'I'll be right out front. Don't take too long.'

I sit on the stainless steel seat, feeling the wild chill. My nose twitches at the smell of urine and a rank bleachy disinfectant. The floor is slick with mysterious moisture. I move my feet apart to escape it. The graffiti on the wall invites me to a fuck and a suck someplace called the North Corner. A phone number begs for me to call, promising a good time and a young hard dick.

A drawing of an erect cock contains so much detail my eyes are drawn to it; the craggy lines on the shaft and veined urethra, the lines detailing the cockhead and hanging balls. The pubic hair is tendril-like, drawn in deep black lines. There's a two-inch hole in the partition and I can't help but look at the seat next to mine. Gloryhole, I think they call it.

This place frightens me. I can't go pee here. I wiggle my legs. Then I feel it. Growing arousal from being in a forbidden place. A place for men discarded only until needed for pleasure and release. I touch the hole in the wall, push my finger through.

Then I hear someone enter the restroom. I panic. Where's Dora? But I'm afraid to cry out. I watch as the man's shoes move quickly to the stall next to mine. I sit back hoping he can't see me, that maybe he'll just piss and go away. But I see his shoes turn and face out, I hear his shorts shuffle off his hips and onto the floor and see them gathered at his ankles. Oh God, where is Dora? He leans forward. I see his clasped hands. He breathes deep. I hear his first tinkle. My pussy's wet and dripping. We are strangers releasing, side by side. He pees a long, hard, very liquid stream that sounds like water from a garden hose. My hands are sweating. I see his hair then his eye appears in the gloryhole. He watches me briefly and coughs. His legs readjust wider; he kicks off his shoes and sheds his shorts. I lean toward the hole. What is he doing? My eyes widen as his cock, long and hard, rises from his crotch as he pumps. I hear his moans and watch his bare feet go up on his tiptoes, then his legs extend. The hole isn't big enough for a good look, so I listen. I wait for his come, but nothing. My cunt thunders as I plunge my fingers inside myself, biting my lip as I, too, rise upon tiptoes and feel the bliss flow over me. I hear his movement as he stands. Then his cock slides through the hole, pulsating. I grab his dick and pump it with my hand.

'Suck it,' he says, the command bounces around the room. Then Dora's disembodied voice floats above me.

'Suck that cock, you little minx.'

I scoot off the toilet seat and take him full in my mouth from a squatting position. I move my lips up and down it, tonguing the slit at the head, and wishing the balls had room to pop through. I jack him with my hand, and hear him groan and sigh in deep, lust-saturated notes. I again take his prick whole with my mouth. He shakes the partition so violently I fear he'll rip it from the floor, but I play his dick until my reward shoots out and runs down my side of the stall.

I need him between my legs. Desperately. I speak into the hole.

'I need you to fuck me, sir, please?'

I'm plunging myself with three crooked fingers, thrusting my breasts, breathing in the rank air of come and disinfectant. I kick off my shoes and feel my bare feet slide on the slick concrete floor. I spread my legs. His eye watches me.

'See, sir? I need to get a good fucking. I'm all dishevelled over here.'

Silence. Then I hear heavy breathing and watch his cock resurrect. I stand and wait until his dick appears then turn away to feel it run between my legs until I put his prick in me, easing back until my ass is flat on the barrier, my pussy filled with my marvellous stranger, then I lean forward, gripping the bowl, as he fucks me with wild, barrier-quaking abandon. I come hard, my toes cramping against the edge of the bowl, my arms stiff and sore from pushing myself onto his prick.

He eases his cock from both holes (giggle), and I sit down and look into the gloryhole, hoping to see his face, but he stands, gathers his clothing and leaves.

Dora calls for me.

'Are you quite done in there?'

'Yes, ma'am,' I reply.

'Was that a good adventure, Pammy?'

'Yes, Dora.'

'Good, Pammy, let's hurry home. I could use a shower.'

Submission in Silk
by Giselle Renarde

'Do you think it's weird that I shave my pussy but I don't shave my legs?'

'What?' Priti shouted over the shower's hiss. 'I didn't catch a word of that.'

Devra closed the toilet lid and climbed on top of it. 'Do you think it's weird that I shave my pussy but not my legs?' Devra repeated, wiping fresh fog from the bathroom mirror to admire her handiwork.

'No,' Priti replied after due consideration. 'I know your leg hair is important to you.'

Chuckling, Devra ran a dye-spotted towel over her sopping-wet hair. 'Yeah, I'm like Samson. My leg hair gives me strength.'

'Well, it kind of does, doesn't it? It's like your lesbian-feminist power source or something,' Priti mused. 'Who's Samson?'

'Seriously?' Devra laughed. 'You don't know the story of Samson and Delilah? Isn't it common knowledge?'

Priti poked her head out from behind the shower curtain, squinting her eyes like she might say *yes*. 'Are they a Bible thing?'

'I can't believe you don't know Samson and Delilah,' Devra marvelled. 'Every kid learns that story. If you don't learn it in Sunday school, you're bound to pick it up *somewhere*.'

'Maybe in this country. Not in mine,' Priti scoffed. 'I hate it when you get all anglo-euro-Christian-centric on me.'

'That is *so* not a word.'

A grin broke across Priti's lips. 'Shut up. Yes it is,' she chuckled, slipping her head back under the showerhead. 'Anyway, we're not going to let religion come between us; that's precisely what *they'd* want.'

Whoever *they* were.

'Why don't I just tell you the story?' Devra suggested, drying between her toes with the spotty towel.

'Oh goody wonderfulness,' Priti sang. 'Gather 'round, all ye filthy pagans. It's Christian storybook time!'

Devra breathed in the heavy floral aroma of the hot shower air. It's not like she was trying to force her beliefs on her girlfriend; it was just a story. 'Knowledge is power.'

'Yes, of course it is, honeyfig,' she sighed. 'If there's one thing I know, it's who holds what rank in our power structure.'

Deciding not to read too much into that comment, Devra continued, 'OK, I'm going to tell you this story, and hopefully you won't accuse me of being ethnocentric – which *is* a real word, by the way. So, the first thing you need to know about Samson is that he was a seriously hairy dude.'

'That much I did already know, thank you,' Priti declared.

'Good. OK,' Devra began, realising she remembered far less of this story than she'd anticipated. 'Right, so Samson was … an Israelite … I think?'

'That I couldn't tell you, hon.'

'I think he was. Anyway, he was a really strong guy. He had superhuman powers because of all his hair – that was the source of his strength. I think his father was like an angel or maybe … no, that doesn't sound right … but there was something about his parents …'

The shower squealed off as Devra searched her brain for the elusive Samson and Delilah file. When Priti pulled the shower curtain open, her focus shifted.

'Holy Christ,' Devra cried, nearly falling off the counter. 'You shaved!'

'You like?' Priti replied with a coy smile, drawing her fingers across wet skin.

'God yes!' she drooled, fixated on that beautifully shaved pussy. 'It looks incredible.'

Priti grabbed the blue towel from the rack and patted down her smooth mound. 'I've never shaved my pussy before ...'

'I know.'

'But you've inspired me, honeyfig,' Priti continued, skimming the towel across her legs and arms. 'The hairless look suits you so well, I thought I should give it a try.'

'Well, the look is only half the story,' Devra cooed, hopping up from the toilet to hang her towel. She took Priti's towel too, draped it around her lover's shoulders, and pulled her close. In their terriclothed embrace, she rubbed Priti's back dry. The brush of Priti's dark nipples against her bare tits sent a shockwave straight to her cunt. Devra's knees nearly gave out at the sensation of clean, goosebumped flesh against flesh.

Hanging Priti's towel on the hook beside the shower, Devra opened the bathroom door. The bedroom beckoned. The atmosphere, the pillows, the luxury linens.

Devra leant against her neatly made bed. Priti leant against Devra. Tits pressing tits, hips brushing hips, they hovered close. The gorgeous girl's subtle breath against Devra's lips invited a kiss. The first kiss was always a little one. Of course, one taste of that sweet warm tongue was never enough. Devra kissed Priti again, gripping her round ass with both hands as they devoured one another's mouths. Taking one step back, Priti smiled, looking a little dazed.

'The best part about a shaved pussy is how it feels to *you*,' Devra whispered, sliding her hand down Priti's curvy stomach to the spot that had never been so bare.

Priti hissed at the sensation. 'It feels so good with your fingers touching me. Even the hot water falling against my skin in the shower felt incredible.'

'I know,' Devra agreed, her eager fingers parting wet lips. As she rubbed pussy juice against that erect clit, Priti grabbed hold of Devra's arm. Her ecstatic eyes rolled back and her mouth opened and closed like a drowning woman gasping for breath. Devra chuckled deep in her throat at the immediacy of her lover's reaction. 'Doesn't everything feel like new?' she asked.

'Yes,' Priti moaned. Rocking her hips, she slid across

Devra's palm.

'Don't you feel like nobody's fingers have ever been here before?' Devra teased, squeezing Priti's pussy lips.

'Oh, yes,' she breathed.

Devra slid onto the bed, leaving Priti to hang in the air like fresh laundry on a clothesline. With her eyes closed, it took a moment or two before Priti seemed to realise she was partnerless.

'I'm over here,' Devra taunted, spreading her naked self across the jacquard bedspread.

'Why?'

With a smirk, Devra replied, 'I was hoping you'd come and join me.'

'Do I have to?' Priti asked with an exaggerated mock-virgin pout. 'I don't know about all this sex stuff ...'

'You know I would never make you do anything you didn't want to do,' Devra assured her, turning down the linens.

'It's not like I could stop you. My hair was my source of strength and now it's all gone,' Priti replied in her characteristic flirty voice.

'You still have hair,' Devra taunted. She reached out to tug on Priti's wet locks, but couldn't quite reach.

'Yes, but the hair from my *pussy* was the power supply.'

'Ah,' Devra nodded in earnest, pretending this exchange was not amusing in the least. Hopping off the bed, she strutted circles around her playful lover. 'Weak and powerless, are you?'

'Yes,' Priti nodded, wide-eyed.

'Unable to defend yourself? At the mercy of my whims?'

'Completely,' she replied, falling to her knees. 'I submit my unwilling body to its fate at your brutal hands.'

'Brutal?' Devra halted her circling. 'You want me to overpower you ...'

'If you must,' the drama queen answered. 'Use and abuse me.'

Rubbing her chin in contemplation, Devra replied, 'Nah.'

Priti's eyes grew wide. Her mouth fell open. 'Excuse me?' she growled, suddenly red-hot. 'What did you just say?'

Devra took two steps back and hopped up on the bed. Leaning into the luxury pillows, she stuck cold toes under the covers and looked down at her fuming partner. 'I said, *no thank you*.'

'Yeah, I got that,' Priti barked. She rose to her feet, folding furious arms across her chest. 'That's real nice, Dev. *Real* nice. I shaved my pussy because I thought it would be something nice for you – for *us* – and what's your reaction? *Thanks, but no thanks. Try being thinner ... and blonder ... and whiter.*'

Devra opened her mouth, but only to draw a deep breath. She propped her head up on another pillow. It wasn't worth arguing just yet. Devra knew how to get herself out of these scrapes. She knew Priti wouldn't listen until she got all her frustration out of her system. Best to wait out the storm.

'You think I didn't notice you checking out the waitress tonight? *Everyone* noticed. Is that what you want? You want a perfect princess Barbie in a short skirt? Fine! You go get her.' Priti wore down the carpet with her frenzied pacing. 'Don't worry. I understand completely. I never knew what you saw in me in the first place. You could do so much better than a big fat Indian nerd.'

Devra tried not to roll her eyes. 'Are you finished?'

'No, I am not finished with you,' she cried, coming to a rest at the foot of the bed. 'Why? Are you finished with me? I knew it would come to this. You need a girl who isn't afraid to hold your hand at the movies. You need a girl who isn't afraid of the word *girlfriend*. See? I know exactly what you need, honeyfig, and I know I'm not it. So that's fine. If you want to find someone else, I understand.'

An impish smile crept across Devra's lips and she patted the mattress, beckoning Priti.

'If you think I'm getting into bed with you, you're crazy. And wipe that smile off your face, will you? This is no time for ...' Priti seemed to be searching for the right word, but finally settled on, 'smiling.'

'I'm sorry, Priti,' Devra cooed. An amused grin was still painted across her face, but she knew she could get away with it. She'd said the magic word: Priti.

It worked every time.

Priti's countenance softened and she snuck up on the bed, curling in like a tabby for Devra to pet. It wasn't that Priti was egomaniacal; she just liked the sound of her own name.

'You don't honestly believe I'd dump you for someone else,' Devra said. It was more a statement than a question.

'No,' Priti conceded. 'I know you wouldn't.' Flipping around to face Devra, she whined, 'But then why did you say no?'

Devra shook her head. Highly entertained by Priti's overly emotional reaction, she challenged, 'Do you even remember what I said no to?'

Pressing her shower-wet head against the pillows, Priti stared up at the light fixture. The question was on her lips. She repeated it back to herself. Finally, 'No.'

'Classic Priti,' Devra laughed. 'You asked me if I wanted to overpower you – to use and abuse you – and I said no.'

'Oh,' she replied. 'Is that really what that was all about?'

'Yes ...'

'Oh.'

'And you didn't want to?'

'No,' Devra chuckled.

Priti's mouth opened then closed, and her brows furled. 'Why not?'

'Do you really have to ask?' Throwing an arm around Priti's waist, Devra traced the outlines of Priti's hips with the tips of her fingernails. 'I don't want to overpower you or use you or abuse you – ever – not even in jest. I want you to give yourself to me *freely*, the way I give myself to you.'

'Are you sure?' Priti pouted, finding enough courage to ask, 'Don't you think it would be fun to play with the power dynamic a little bit?'

'I think that's fun for some people, certainly,' Devra replied, 'but it's not for me.'

Priti stared at the ceiling as Devra's gaze followed the line of her forehead down across her nose, the curve of her lips, and her chin, down the slope of neck ...

'OK,' Priti replied, folding her hands behind her head. This simple move was code: Devra now had unhindered access to Priti's luscious breasts.

'We can submit to each other without anybody dominating anybody,' Devra explained, licking circles around Priti's nipples and blowing on them. They stood at attention, beckoning her lips. 'It's simultaneous submission, Priti – you give yourself to me and I give myself to you.'

'And it's in giving that we receive, right?' Priti asked. That was Devra's motto.

'Yes, exactly!' Devra cheered. 'Wait, are you making fun of me?'

'A little bit.'

'But it's so true,' she said, taking little bites at Priti's nipples. 'I get off more on giving you head than getting it.'

'Yeah, but that's because you're weird,' Priti replied, pressing Devra's head against her breasts. 'And because I'm not very good at giving head.'

'No self-deprecation in this bed,' Devra scolded, her words muffled by two large tits. She licked and licked and sucked at that fine flesh as she cooed, 'I love what you do. You are the most alluring, arousing, talented woman in the world.'

'I'd say you're biased.'

'So?' Devra teased, pressing her thigh against Priti's delicate mound. Priti gasped. Throwing her head back against the mountain of pillows, she sparked an avalanche of satin and cotton batting. The two women were suddenly buried beneath Devra's immense cushion collection.

With a flirty giggle, Priti dug Devra out. 'Is this one new?' she asked, setting a light blue neck roll under her chin.

'You're supposed to put it *under* your neck, not on top of it,' Devra chuckled, grabbing it away. 'Yes, this is my latest acquisition.'

Playfully tapping Devra's head with one of many cushions, she teased, 'I've never met anyone who collects pillows.'

'Yes you have; you've met me,' Devra laughed. Stealing the neck roll from Priti's hands, she ran the smooth cushion down the front of Priti's body. 'This one is pure silk.'

Priti sharply inhaled as the neck roll's sumptuous texture

met her shaved pussy. 'I can tell,' she said. Almost imperceptibly, her hips began to writhe against the smooth silk. 'Oh, wow ...'

Splayed like a leaping frog, Devra set her weight down against Priti and the fine pillow. The slick sensation of silk against her smooth lips made her growl as she wrapped her legs around Priti's.

'Ohhh ...' Priti sighed, jutting her chest forward. 'I love silk ...'

'Isn't it just the purest feeling in the world – a freshly shaved pussy against 100 per cent silk?'

Pinning Priti's shoulders to the bed, Devra trapped her curvy girl in place. She stroked her own throbbing pussy lips against the cushion. The liquid silk of her body met with the glossy fabric to make for a super-slick ride. Priti writhed beneath her, tribbing on the flipside of the pillow.

'How's this feel?' Devra asked, stroking her wet cunt against the silk as she held Priti's shoulders down.

'Oh,' Priti cried, as if she were surprised by how amazing it felt. 'So good ...' Though she was pinned under her partner, Priti still managed to take hold of Devra's hard nipples and squeeze. 'How's *this*?' she teased.

'Yes ...' Devra hissed. 'That is *so good*.'

With crimson fingernails, Priti pinched her tits. Devra moaned, tribbing harder against the silk cushion. Squealing at the pressure, Priti thrust in response. Her face was especially beautiful when she was about to come, pink cheeks puffing and lips red with arousal. 'How do you like this?' Priti hissed, twisting Devra's hard nipples in tight circles.

The pleasure stung. She knew she'd be feeling it for days, but she didn't care. 'Yes, that's good!' Devra cried. 'Harder!'

Priti twisted her nipples, pulling on Devra's small tits. Devra slid back and forth against the neck roll between their legs. The stroke of silk against her pussy lips beautifully complemented the sharp pain of being hauled around by her breasts. Those fingernails hurt like hell, and she loved it.

Shutting her eyes tight, Priti bucked up hard. Had their legs not been so thoroughly entangled, she would have sent Devra flying across the bed. She pounded her clit against the sopping silk. Without the cushion as a buffer, their pussies would have been broken and bruised by the intensity of their movements.

Priti's sweet cries roused Devra to a frenzied state. As Priti's little yips and hollers sounded increasingly like actual words, Devra realised she was uttering her catchphrase, 'Say my name.'

Devra chuckled to herself. *Predictable Priti.* Looking down at her girl's beautiful round face, she growled, 'Priti, you are *so fucking hot*!'

Priti squealed orgasmically. Clinging to Devra's legs, she pulled her down by the tits for an out-of-this-world kiss. It was the sort of moment so cosmic, she would never recollect it with complete accuracy. All she could do now was to give herself over to the full experience in this moment. Later she would remember it as an instant of perfect bliss.

As she lay on top of ecstatic Priti, tangled in limbs, Devra rolled gently to extract the molested neck roll from between their exhausted bodies. She settled back down against her gorgeous girlfriend, and Priti mumbled, 'See? What did I tell you?'

'About what?' Devra asked.

'Someone is always in control,' she sighed with an air of utter contentment. 'You were on top, dominating me ...'

Devra smiled, setting her head down beside Priti's. 'That's strange. I was about to say *you* were the dominant one, leading me around by the tits.'

'What would you call the flipside of simultaneous submission?' Priti mused.

Devra contemplated the terminology. 'Dual domination?' she laughed. 'I don't know. Sex makes me stupid.'

'Me too,' Priti sighed. Devra ran her fingers over Priti's warm breasts.

'Hey, I just remembered something,' Devra said with a flinch. 'Samson ... the hairy dude ... he fought as an insurgent against the Philistines. His enemies saw him as a threat because he was so strong. They needed to acquire intelligence on him by any means necessary.'

'Oh,' Priti breathed, either in reflection or boredom.

'Samson fell in love with this chick Delilah, but his enemies got to her first. They bribed her to find out the secret of his strength. He didn't want to tell her, so she guilt-tripped him by doing that whole *if you really loved me you wouldn't keep secrets* thing. He told her, of course. What choice did he have? The source of his strength was his hair. That's why he never cut it.'

'OK.'

'One night after he fell asleep, Delilah cut off all his hair and his enemies nabbed him. He was in prison so long waiting for trial that by the time they brought him into the courtroom, his hair had grown back and he was powerful again. He knocked down the pillars of the courthouse and the whole damn place collapsed. It killed the Philistine judges, but it killed Samson too.'

Cuddling in against Devra, Priti mused, 'That's what I hate about the Bible: every woman is a femme fatale.'

Devra contemplated arguing that the Holy Virgin was in no way a femme fatale – she was the Queen of Heaven, damn it, and people across the globe worshipped her – but was it really worth fighting about? Priti was entitled to her opinion.

'I guess you're right,' Devra conceded. Of course, this concession fell on deaf ears. Priti was sound asleep. With a smile on her lips, Devra wrapped her arms around her girl and snuggled in beside her.

Go Find Yourself
by Velvet Tripp

The drive had taken nearly five hours and by the time I reached the camp it was already dark. Motorway traffic had turned my three-hour journey of discovery into a five-hour crawl of anticipation and frustration. Thank goodness I'd graduated from a tent to my camper van. Once I'd found a good spot to park and put down the stabilisers, I could climb in the back of my camper and make a hot drink.

At last. I was here. The trip I'd been looking forward to since I'd found out about this very special camp three months ago.

The last few years had been mayhem. My partner of 15 years found himself a newer, younger model to go with his XJ6 and this year my son had gone off to university, leaving me free to pursue my own interests for the first time in years. Lonely nights of sorrow had had their revealing moments. Memories had taken me back to my teenage years. To times when I would lie awake at night fantasising about women. And sex. Back then it was still taboo. Women didn't do that sort of thing, did they? And if they did they were scorned. Outcast. Too different.

I remembered one time going home from a dance. Music and dance had always meant a lot to me, and I'd seen a live band I loved and danced all evening, but at 17 I still had to get the bus home. So there I stood, waiting at the bus station. A girl not much older than me stood further down, waiting for a Number 34. She had short, sleek black hair cut into the nape of her neck. Her chiselled features and cute, pouting lips suited the cut, and her figure – equally slim and chic – was dressed in boyish jeans and a low-cut T-shirt that showed just enough cleavage. The whole look was topped with a denim jacket. I couldn't help but notice her, reading her novel while casually leaning on the queue barrier.

She must have sensed my stare and glanced up straight at me. I quickly looked away but it was too late. She smiled and began walking towards me. My heart jumped in fear. I forced a smile but must have looked nervous. 'It's OK, I won't bite. Unless you want me to, of course,' the girl said, smiling. 'Come on, let's walk.' I don't know what got into me. I followed her to the small, tree-lined square close by. She stopped under a willow tree and leant provocatively against its trunk.

Up close she was stunning. And she smelt delicious, like musk and roses. She tasted even more delicious, when we kissed. I was transfixed. Before I knew what was happening, her hand was under my top, caressing my breast, stirring my nipple into life. When she began pushing her hip into my pussy and I realised how much I wanted her I freaked. Lost it. Coward that I was, I took flight back to the bus station, jumping on the first bus going in my direction that came in. I'd had fantasies about that girl. Wished I'd had the courage to stay in the square and let things take their course. I would always wonder what it would be like to go home with her, get naked with her. But Daddy wouldn't have approved, and I was a good girl.

Now I was at the other end of the country, 20 something years on, and I'd done the conventional thing. Raised a child, been a faithful partner in a straight marriage and ended up alone. Times had changed. Attitudes had changed. Lesbians were out and proud, in force. And I was sick of hiding from myself.

So here I was, at ACCN – the Alternative Camp from Cultural Norms. There was still a lot of prejudice around, and a camp like this could have attracted the wrong kind of press and public attention, so the acronym worked to keep them away. I'd been passed the contact details by a friend in whom I'd confided, sent off my form and camp fees. Now, here I was. I knew no one.

While the kettle boiled, I changed into a warmer jacket. It was July, but the nights still got chilly and I had no plans to huddle in my van alone. I surveyed the site. Down in the lower part of the camp I could see a large welcoming fire. Lots of people appeared to be sitting around and the sound of drumming drifted towards me on the cool night air. Sipping my tea, I felt a rising sense of anticipation in my gut. How would a bunch of out-and-proud gays and lesbians take to a middle-aged coward of a woman? I was sure they wouldn't appreciate the fact they'd been fighting the fight while I'd played housewife all these years. By the time my teacup was empty, I'd decided to keep my past to myself.

Slowly making my way across the field, the sight of my new acquaintances-to-be suddenly filled me with fear. I stood motionless and breathed deeply. This was an old fear, buried deep, based in other people's prejudice and my own lack of confidence. 'Hi,' a voice from behind me said. I jumped. The voice laughed. 'Sorry to startle you. You new?'

'Erm, yes. I just thought I'd go down to the fire. Introduce myself.'

She had a torch and, in the dim light, I could see I was talking to a 30-something woman with long blonde hair. She held out a hand.

'Come on then. This field is a bit treacherous. It's the tussock-grass. I've already hit the deck twice,' she chuckled. 'The name's Babs.'

Babs was brilliant. It turned out she was here with her partner of nearly eight years and made me feel welcome. No one was too nosey, so it wasn't long before I'd relaxed and started to chat away to people. The sight by the fire was one to behold. There were men in gorgeous dresses and skirts, girls stripped to the waist dancing and even someone enjoying a back massage on the grass by the fire. But one woman stood out from the crowd. She had short dark hair, deliciously dark brown eyes and the type of slim, androgynous body that had me drooling. She was drumming. Someone explained the hand-held drum that looked like a tambourine was a bodhran. Her fingers skimmed over its skin to the rhythm set by the bigger, bassier drums. The bangle on her wrist glinted in the firelight, echoing the light in her eyes, which appeared to dance and laugh as she played.

I was enthralled. She was stunning. Surely I wouldn't stand a chance. She must be here with someone, and even if she wasn't, despite keeping trim all these years, my looks could never compete with hers. My imagination began to toy with me again. I could envisage myself in her arms, skin to skin, kissing those luscious lips.

Next day, having slept fitfully and dreaming of the drummer girl, I wandered down to the main marquee. Groups of people were huddled around, drinking coffee, chatting, smoking. Hah, they can't legislate for a field, I thought rebelliously, and lit my own, plonking myself down on a conveniently placed rug. 'Hi again,' a voice said. I turned.

'Morning, Babs. Sleep well?'

'Yeah, fine.'

It was then I noticed the others in her group. Janine, her partner, Geoff, without last night's glam makeover – and drummer girl!

'Lisa, this is Ross. She came down with us from Cumbria. Drummer, dancer and solicitor.'

Ross beamed. 'Hi,' she said, squatting on the rug next to me. 'Mind if we join you?'

'Please,' I said gesturing to the others.

The rest of the day was a dream. Ross and I really hit it off. She was smart, funny *and* extremely sexy. For someone who had spent two nights in a field, she smelt fantastic too. She'd gone off to help make a communal meal with her friends, and I'd prepared food to re-heat for today, so we were meeting later by the fire. Now I was nervous. Would she want me? Could I go through with it if she did?

By the fire, Ross had saved me a seat by hers, ready for the drumming to start. Wine was flowing, people were singing, clapping, dancing, and for a while I joined them, feeling all the constraints of my "normal" life falling away. The throbbing of the drums was a constant reminder of the throbbing between my legs each time I looked at Ross. Eventually "drum curfew" time arrived, after which everything, for the sake of neighbouring farms, had to be quietened down. The night continued with chatting, laughing people sat in groups huddled around the fire, and I shivered a little as the night air brushed my skin.

'Time for a nightcap?' Ross asked.

'Yeah. Would you like to come back to my patch?'

She nodded. We wandered back up the field, my heart thumping so loud in my chest I feared she would be able to hear it. My camper is very small. A two-person mini job with all the basics – a fridge, cooker and sink, water tank and double bed. Once I'd made hot chocolate laced with brandy to warm us, the heat from the cooker had warmed the space.

'I was hoping you'd invite me back,' Ross said. 'I saw you walking down to the fire with Babs last night, but I was committed to help with the drumming. The other bodhran players only arrived today.'

I was surprised, but delighted. 'I thought you'd probably be with someone.'

'No, alone for the past nine months. I've been too busy with work to go out much. But I have plenty of time now.' She beamed, leaning towards me.

I put down my mug. That first sweet kiss is one I'll never, ever forget. The heady scent of her filled my nostrils as we embraced. As her soft, sweet lips touched mine tiny bolts of lightning shot through my body. When her tongue met mine the lightning grew, expanded. As we drew closer and her breasts pushed against mine I was on fire. Nothing in my imagination had prepared me for the sensual delights of kissing a beautiful woman. And the night was very young. She drew back, stroking my long auburn hair. 'You're new, aren't you?' she asked.

'Yep,' I confessed. 'First time I've ever been to a camp like this.'

'No, I mean you're new to this scene.'

'How did you know?' I frowned.

'Shhh, it doesn't matter. Now how does this bed go together?' she replied, smiling, gazing gently into my eyes.

It took less than five minutes to convert the seating into my bed. Once the sheets were on and the quilt and pillows in place, it made for a very cosy space. I reached into the cupboard above us and opened some wine, pouring two glasses. My mind was racing, my hands shaking. Nerves had begun to get to me. No experience. It came back to that. She didn't give me time to worry about it and, taking the glasses, she placed them on the side out of the way then leant back on a pillow.

'Come here,' she beckoned with her finger.

I leant across to her and she took me in her arms again. And again came the lightning. It was a buzz of utter magic that blew my mind. We kissed, long and hard this time, with more passion than I'd ever known. Why had I waited so long? Her hands explored my body, stroking over my breasts, finding her way under my jumper. This was too much! I quickly tore the jumper over my head as she unclipped my bra. Her hands cupped my naked breasts, and she kissed and sucked each nipple in turn. I groaned softly and fell back on the pillows. She pulled her own jumper off, revealing her small pert breasts that needed no bra for them to look perfect. Soon we were naked, kissing passionately and exploring each other's bodies. This felt so right. So good. Sex with my ex had been OK, but never more than just that. With Ross everything felt so right.

'Got any massage oil?' she asked me.

I reached into the cupboard and dug out the patchouli-scented oil I loved. She started on my back, sensuously working the oil into my skin, fingers stroking over my shoulder blades, down the centre of my back and up my spine to my neck, stopping briefly to kiss my ear. I shivered in anticipation. Then she turned me over and began slowly working her way down from my neck and over my shoulders, down my chest and over my breasts, ensuring every stroke of her fingers left me ever more breathless. The oil felt wonderful as she teased my nipples with her lubricated fingers, a feeling like silk trailing over them, and they stood proud and erect for her. She

114

looked approvingly down at them, smiled and continued down, working the oil over my belly, trailing the occasional nail and leaving me gasping. Dragging her fingers over my hip bones, round the magic triangle of my mons, inside my thighs, teasing, dancing her fingers over my body as skilfully as she played the bodhran. Then she crawled up my body, rubbing herself against me, her nipples hard as little rocks, pushing into me as she moved. We tangled again, kissing passionately, sliding against each other. My van had never been so hot; by now the windows were steamed up.

Her gentle fingers continued to caress me in ways I'd never felt before, building sensations that electrified my skin, lit up my excitement and made my head spin. We took our sweet time. Her mouth explored my breasts, teasing each nipple in turn and kissed her way down over my belly, over my navel and down to my pleading pussy. As her tongue expertly delved ever deeper into my folds she found my clit, and it too was on fire, firm and throbbing. With even strokes, she slowly built the pressure then pushed a finger inside me, and another.

I was heaving to meet her, pushing myself into her, gasping as she sent me higher, beyond control of thought or movement, just response. As she licked my clit and delved deep into my slit the world melted away as I found myself floating in ecstasy, riding the waves of the best climax of my life, thrusting eager hips at my gorgeous lover.

It was a while before I regained my composure. Ross stroked my hair, cuddled and kissed me until I was able to speak. 'Wonderful,' was all I could say. She smiled. That feeling was heaven, bliss. I was happier than I'd ever been with anyone anywhere. Still naked, we lounged around with our wine, sipping slowly, savouring the flavour, drinking in the experience. Now I wanted to give Ross the same pleasure she had given me.

I turned and kissed her, gently at first, then harder, more insistent. Now she moaned with pleasure. I kissed her neck, shoulders, stroked my fingers down her back, over her buttocks. She shivered. I took one hard little nipple into my mouth, running my tongue over it, feeling it harden even more.

As I nibbled a little, she moaned again. I carried on, switching my attention to the other nipple, and at the same time moving my hands down to her pussy. Gently stroking her pubes, I found my way slowly to her clit. Massaging it in gently circling motions, I felt it harden. I could resist no more, and pushed my tongue between her folds, tasting her as she rocked her hips towards me. I took my time, lapping her sweet juices as they ran, loving every second. After a long delicious time, she came in my mouth, writhing with pleasure, breathing hard. I felt the pulse of her come, revelled in the delights of discovery I had made that night.

Next morning, I woke next to Ross, still sleeping. She looked as beautiful asleep as she had the night before. Quietly, I crawled to the end of the bed and started coffee. It wasn't long before the smell wakened her. We took our time sipping coffee and eating breakfast, still propped up in my bed.

'Ross,' I said, after a while. 'What told you I was new? I mean, I hadn't told a soul here.'

'Body language, but don't worry about it. We all had to have a first time, didn't we?'

'Yeah, but at my age?'

'It's more common than you think, you know. Lots of people try to be straight. And who can blame them, especially as it's still a world of prejudice.'

'It's better now than it was 20 years ago. And you didn't do the straight route.'

'Who told you that? I was married for two years. But he was a shit. So it didn't take me that long to get out of it and rethink.'

'You have any kids?'

'No, or it wouldn't have been so easy.'

'I had a son. He's grown now, left home.'

'There you go. No wonder it took you so long. Don't worry, I won't hold it against you,' she laughed.

There was still a week left on the camp. Each day was filled with walks in the fields, making new friends, laughing, eating. The evenings by that fire were wonderful, joy-filled times of dance and drums, singing and laughter. But the nights. They meant I didn't see dawn apart from the one night that Ross and I went for a walk before we slept. The nights were the best of my life, a joyous journey of self discovery and wish fulfilment.

As the last hot night of the campest camp I'd ever imagined came to a close and Ross and I sat naked in my van sipping our brandy chocolate, I began to fear leaving. Going back to my old life was, at that moment, unthinkable. I frowned.

Ross looked at me, concerned. 'What is it, honey?'

'I, erm, don't want to go home. Stupid, I know.'

'We will be able to see each other again, won't we?' she asked.

The relief flooded through me. I had fallen for this woman in a big way, and hadn't wanted to admit it, even to myself. But when she said that, well, I knew for sure what I wanted.

I turned and kissed her passionately. 'We're only 60 miles apart, and what's 60 miles? I travelled over 250 to get here, and enjoyed the ride.'

Ross laughed. 'Well, enjoy this one,' she said, picking up her bodhran. She began to drum a slow, pulsing beat, swinging her hips in front of me, a sexy smile on her lips. I lay back and listened as she performed in private for me. I watched her nimble fingers dance their way over the drum skin, imagining them making the same delicate moves on my skin. Her hips gyrated even more as she saw the effect she was having on me. In the warmth of the camper, her scent drifted into my nostrils, her pert nipples only inches from my face. I groaned, managing to croak, 'You don't work seven days a week, do you?'

Ross laughed. 'I work hard, but not that damn hard. Besides, I was only working 24/7 because I had nothing better to do. Now I have something far more important to spend my time on,' she replied, running her fingers through my hair. I shivered with delight. She leant forward, and our lips met again. Skin on skin, we made the most of that last night on camp.

'My place next weekend then?' Ross murmured as we curled up hours later. 'I'm sure I can find some way to entertain you …'

The Girl from Xanadu
by Olivia London

The phrase "opposites attract" always struck me as trite until I met Velma Guile. I was toiling at a Bay Area law firm, ostensibly as a proof-reader but mostly as a factotum arriving early to churn buckets of thick gourmet coffee, leaving late to make sense of the baritone bafflegab on the tapes I was hired to transcribe. I was a working-class worker bee, brought into this world to earn my bread buttered on one side.

Velma worked to have something to do. Her grandfather had invented a widget of some sort and the trickle-down theory of wealth created for VG a lifelong trough from which to draw funds. She pouted her way to SF with a Southern name and a charming Southern accent, but everything else about this exotic transplant betokened a highly charged, albeit aimless ambition and a soigné sophistication that left men *and* women panting in her swivel-hipped path.

She started out at Smith, Smitty, Smitty & Fife as an unpaid intern performing tasks which might be expected from an unnecessary or catatonic employee. From what I could glean, her job consisted of shopping at high-end stores for gewgaws Charlie Fife needed to appease a greedy mistress and long lunches with Old Man Smitty, the senior Smitty at 3SF.

It was after one of these long lunches at Café Brioche that VG decided to get acquainted with a member of the proletariat.

'Here,' she cooed, plopping a paisley-patterned paper bag on my desk.

'I don't want your cassoulet leftovers,' I said, not bothering to look up.

Velma leant over my desk, dangerously close, so close I could smell her floral perfume and reach, if I dared, for a sip of happiness already pouring from her garnet-painted lips.

'I'd never bring you hand-me-down food, Claire. Besides, the cassoulet at Café B is frightful. You work so hard. Thought I'd bring you some sustenance to keep you peddling down that path of thankless travail.'

I looked in the bag then peered again. This is why you move to San Francisco: crab cakes resting like Monet's *Water Lilies* in the palms of braised endive. Asparagus so verdant and tender they look almost velveteen. Enter the most pedestrian diner and the horror of your mother's desiccated potatoes becomes someone else's nightmare as you bite into an omelette bursting with brie and grilled vegetables. This is a city where salmon is the new chicken and aioli is the condiment of choice.

'Oh, well. Thanks, Velma.' I sighed, knowing I could never reciprocate such generosity.

When she straightened I couldn't help but notice the full sensual shapes filling the mighty precipice of her underwire bra. Through the sheer fabric of her blouse, her nipples solicited touch, prominent as they were like the push buttons in our building's Old World elevators.

I don't remember how it happened that I yielded inexorably and wholeheartedly to the louche milieu of this effervescent gin fizz of femaleness. Like most things, it was a case of gradual attrition … like watching your footprint disappear in wet sand.

The season of my undoing had crested just past fall and the shops in Union Square were already decorated for Christmas. I passed Saks and Tiffany's every day after work to catch one of the two buses I took to get home. My coffee-saturated breath frosted the glass of these stores as I gazed nonplussed at the tony shoppers. Who spent thousands of dollars on a paperweight or a year's proof-reader's salary on an anklet? My heart sank as I answered my own question. Velma Guile frequented these boutiques, often leaving with parcels while wearing the latest Burberry fashions.

She was becoming more tantalising by the moment, and not

just due to her fancy threads and heartbreakingly beautiful looks. There was a vulnerability about this woman that made me want to take her in my arms and cosset her with kisses.

Once, I came upon VG in the employee lounge, brushing a tear from her daintily rouged cheek.

'Why does everyone hate me?' she asked, without preamble.

'What do you mean?' I put my palm on her shoulder in a spontaneous gesture of camaraderie. The soft muscle was like a warm bun in my hand.

'Mrs Standish looks right through me, refusing to answer my questions. Melissa and Carlyle giggle whenever I say Smith, Smitty, Smitty & Fife, like I'm just a big joke or something.'

My expression softened into one of infinite patience and understanding, tinged with a degree of lust. 'Mrs Standish is only nice to people she *has* to be nice to; she's been here so long she doesn't have to be pleasant to anyone. And no one refers to this firm as Smith, Smitty, Smitty & Fife. We all call it 3SF.' Despite my pash, I thought: *You'd know that if you had an actual job here.*

'Thanks, Claire,' she said, taking my hand in hers.

After that, we started hanging out together doing girlie things. I took out a stack of credit cards to keep up with the princess from Xanadu.

On our days off from 3SF, we simply *had* to go for English tea service, and I simply *had* to treat sometimes lest I feel like a mooch.

My schmatte curtain Irish sensibilities balked at the prices. $50 for tea, scones and Devonshire cream? Can anything *clotted* really be good for you?

After our excursions, Velma rewarded me with a squeeze here or a peck there. I wanted more. Much more.

My best friend at the time was an Italian painter Michelangelo would have loved to meet. One night, Tony practically frogmarched me to a bar called Girl Meets Girl and left me there to *mingle*. His word. My agony.

'Stay with me,' I begged, tugging the sleeve of his torn

leather jacket.

'Claire, I'm going to take that carapace of yours and toss it off the Golden Gate Bridge. I brought you here because you're not the type to walk into a bar alone. You look great; now, go get some girlie girl. If you need me, I'll be across the street at The Sun, but not for long!'

I watched my friend's gazelle-like figure depart, secretly coveting the graceful hips which, in a just world, would have belonged to me.

A waitress glided into being and I ordered a Bloody Shame, not yet ready to commit to alcohol. This was definitely the classiest lesbian bar I had seen since moving to Mecca. The redbrick walls featured black-and-white Mapplethorpe-inspired art. Tables were covered with linens of a fine brocade. Not a neon mammary or two-bit game pool table in sight.

I shouldn't have been surprised to see Velma but there she was, draped coquettishly over the bar while a woman with a salon-bought tan chatted her up. I should have left without making a scene but prudence isn't my strong suit. I walked up to the bar ignoring Amazon Woman.

'Hello, Ms Guile. Your last name suits you by the way.'

Looking uncomfortable, VG motioned for her date to step away from the bar. 'Vanna, would you excuse us for a moment?'

'Sure thing, hon.'

Velma gave me a pout and said, 'Claire, don't be jealous. You're not into the bar scene. I am. Plus, the drinks here are a little pricey.' She shuddered on my behalf.

'I let you into the 3SF Club and talked Mrs Standish into giving you a mailbox so you'd feel like a staff member instead of whatever the hell it is you are. I listen to the petty problems keeping your life afloat. Do I mean *anything* to you?'

'Claire, of course you mean the world to me. It's just, well, sometimes I'm only comfortable around people who have a lot of money.'

'Ha! Sometimes I'm only comfortable around people who have a brain.'

VG's big blue eyes widened in surprise mixed with

mischief. 'I'd call you a bitch for that but I wouldn't want to make you cry.'

'I'd call you a flibbertigibbet but I wouldn't want to make you step away from a mirror long enough to look up the meaning of the word. Instead, I'll just call you a bitch.'

There it was: that spandex-stretched moment of tension where you either want to kill your love interest or boff her brains out. I'm a lover not a killer so I naturally opted for the latter course.

'You don't hate me, do you? I can handle antipathy from anyone but you, Claire.'

'Hate you? Velma, if we were to have sex right now, it'd be fantastic.'

'Ooh, what are we waiting for?'

'Want to invite Vanna for a threesome?'

'Don't be naughty. Unless it's with me.'

Vanna had her back to us anyway, getting comfortable with a petite blonde.

We hailed a cab to Velma's condo in North Beach. It was VG's slumming abode away from the Beaux Arts crafted home in Twin Peaks left to her by a childless aunt. I thought we would just hold hands in the backseat but Velma pulled me toward her in a way that made me melt into her embrace. She kissed me softly at first, tenderly planting morsels of affection along the corners of my mouth and chin. Then she parted my lips with her tongue and probed my palette with such a slow but deliberate intensity, I had to do something with my hands to keep them from trembling.

I cupped and fondled her bountiful breasts but soon I was parting her thighs to warm my hands by the fire. Her pussy was warm and wet like a drenched little animal. I tried to be gentle but Velma pressed my index finger to her clit and had me press down hard, then harder until she was guiding my digits down into the crevasse of her desire and telling me to fuck her with my fingers.

The driver was paying us no mind, but I let my coat provide a mantle for us so I could pleasure my date with abandon. Once I had us sequestered, I pushed two fingers into Velma's

123

welcoming folds, then three fingers and, as I gave her what she wanted, I felt my own desire reach a fever pitch; I had never been so wet.

We reached her condo in a lust-filled haze. VG pressed some bills on the driver, telling him to keep the change. He left without a word or a glance at his horny passengers. We ran up a short flight of stairs and headed for the nearest horizontal surface. My last girlfriend had had a waterbed and I was so glad VG's bedroom sported a real mattress. It was firm enough to bounce on like a trampoline and I was ready for some acrobatic lovemaking.

'What were you saying back in the cab, Velma? I don't think I heard you.'

V flipped her long black tresses away from the ample bosom straining against taut fabric and unzipped her requisite little black cocktail dress. She reached behind her back and unsnapped her strapless bra. The sight of those prominent nipples jutting from the dollhouse pink of her areolae literally took my breath away. She placed my hand on one breast while guiding my mouth to the other.

Her tits tasted like powdered sugar doughnuts and I licked and teased her nipples until they resembled thimble-sized servings of grenadine.

I was kissing her ribcage and smooching my way south when V pulled me up to within an inch of her lovely face.

'I was saying,' she murmured in my ear while pressing my hand into service, 'I was saying fuck me, Claire. Fuck me with your fingers, please.'

And so I started pushing my way into her again, pumping her with two, then three fingers, pulling out occasionally to tease the deckled edge of her clit as she bucked and writhed with pleasure. She had come twice in a row like two thunderclaps, but she was wild. She was insatiable. So I fucked her with my other hand while deep kissing her luscious mouth and fondling her delicate nipples. She came again and again until the entire room was permeated with our desire and I could smell nothing but the fluids of our sex, not even the gardenia-based perfume she wore which can make a person swoon from a block away.

When she went down on me I saw not the blank canvas of her ceiling but the colours of our lovemaking: claret-daubed lips, rose petals set free, indigo sheets with a magnificently high thread count.

Soon, all I could do was feel. I closed my eyes and basked in the wonders of a woman's love. Velma hoisted my hips for fast access to my quim and soon her lips were moving in tandem faradizing my clit with such perfect rhythm I thought I might break from the joy she was giving me. Wave after wave overtook me as my lover's tongue prodded and pampered my vulva. That languet alone could have moved a mountain or uncovered a forgotten city.

It's amazing how many times a woman can come with the right lover. And Velma was the perfect lover for me, at least physically. Our bodies presented themselves as feasts and one couldn't get to the table fast enough to devour the other.

Falling asleep in Velma's arms felt like the most natural thing in the world. I woke to a nosegay of womanly scents: powder, perfume, shampoo, the best sheets money can buy and frolicsome pussy.

Velma stretched like a cat and I stroked her belly until she started to purr. I was already moist from the dreams I had of her throughout the night. I kissed her brow and tenderly stroked her back. I fondled her orbs with their dainty nipples like fallen petals, her breasts jutting forward as if arranged nicely on a shelf. Such great cymbals of flesh inspired percussive movement and I determinedly sloothered my minx from her slumber.

I did this by drawing V's vulva to my lips as if it were a jorum from which I'd have my fill. I alternated the mobility of my mouth with faradizing fingers, stimulating her pip patiently but relentlessly until I found her sweet spot and had V thrashing in the sheets as if she were trying to make an angel in the snow.

I plunged into the fluids of her sex, my hands chameleons now in the service of Sapphic love, with the ability to offer the power of a vibrator in one instant and the graceful deft touch of a feather in the next.

'Oh, Claire. Come here, love. If I have one more orgasm I'll pop like a piñata.'

And so I curled into Velma's sated womanly embrace, content in my role as lover which is that of a giver. We cuddled and kissed and languidly caressed each other until reaching that inevitable timberline where even the newest lovers are forced to retreat back into the world.

When I suggested we enjoy breakfast in bed, V's sweet lips pursed into a moue.

'I don't have a coffee pot,' she confessed. 'And I don't know how to cook. I just buy what I need. Too bad we can't order room service.'

'We can't order room service because you don't live in a hotel. Velma, do you really eat out every single meal?'

V shrugged defensively and said, 'Yeah, so. I can do what I want. Don't expect me to apologise for that.'

So we alighted on a café for quiche and cappuccino. Velma's eyes scanned the crowd of the trendy restaurant, occasionally sparkling in recognition or hapless remembrance.

'Oh, there's Jill something-or-other. Now where do I know her from? Oh, yeah. I was an intern at another law firm. She's a legal aide, I think.'

'Did you ever consider law school, V?'

'Oh, yeah. Daddy made me go but I failed the bar twice. Thought I'd try acting but I don't want to worry about my weight. I don't know, Claire. It's a beautiful day. Let's not stress about careers right now. I just want to be with you. OK?'

Trust fund babies are different from you and me I would say to my next lover. *They have a lot more time to think about the things they don't want to do.*

'OK, Velma. We'll take this one caviar canapé at a time. I love being with you.'

We lasted six months. VG tired of doing "this and that" at 3SF and drifted to Europe to study art history. My friends now shake their heads at this story saying I wasted too much time with a flibbertigibbet. But I've never regretted Velma. In the end, all we have are our memories.

And how can anyone forget a trip to Xanadu?

Acid Orange
by Helen Dring

The bath was reassuringly scalding, and I was lying with only my eyes and my hands exposed to the cold air. Above my head, I held an old copy of an Amélie Nothomb novel, wondering why it was every book of hers I'd ever read ended with someone killing themselves. It wasn't how I had always envisaged spending my last day on Earth.

We'd heard the news that morning, the newsbots deadpan as only robots can be. Lee's pager had gone off seconds later, and we'd looked at each other with the frantic "uh-oh" we always feel when the emergency pager beeps. So she'd wriggled into her fatigues and locked her guns, kissed me through my hair and rushed out of the door. Which was why I was in the bath, wrinkling like a raisin and waiting for her to come back.

It's become a bit of a ritual, this. Every time an emergency call goes out, every time she has to leave, I plant myself in the bath with an old-fashioned sci-fi novel and a single cigarette. If she doesn't come back, I plan to smoke the cigarette and plunge myself under the water. If she does, she'll open the bathroom door, pluck me from the bath and towel me dry. Today, I wasn't sticking to the old ritual. I figured I may as well watch the chaos, the final fallout of the surge.

There had been trouble brewing for a long time, even longer than the five years I'd had access to secret information thanks to my emergency corps girlfriend. It had started with the short circuits, the steady decay of the robots that kept things functioning. No one really knew what had caused it. All I knew was that there was too much electricity instead of not enough, and that excess had to go somewhere.

So it exploded as lightning, fires, sudden flashes of heat and terror. Robots, of course, were the most at risk, but it wasn't unusual for a human to switch the light on and unleash seven shades of hell into their own hand. We were scared, and that meant that diplomacy began to fail everywhere, or so it seemed. England went to war over Japan, blaming them for the whole surge crisis because of their robot obsession. Other countries followed, and now it was impossible to keep up with.

I stopped bothering. Our state kept to itself, our emergency corps working all the hours God sent to try and eliminate the surge. It was in vain, and sometimes, when Lee came home with fresh burns across her face and body, enough anger welled within me to cause a surge myself.

The world had been dying for decades. Lee was part of the final resuscitation, breathing what life she could into the decaying compounds that she went to rescue. I envied her strength. I gave relief to no one. I holed myself up in the apartment and pretended I was an old-fashioned housewife. I waited for her to come back, because all the world's problems, all of the anger, everything seemed to stop when Lee came home.

Of course, despite the fact that the world was ending, we had to try to keep calm. Anger only accelerated the surge, made it more potent when it exploded. Which was why I was submerged in the bath, trying to keep my mind on some retro French sci-fi. Trying not to let the synapses in my body connect too viciously. I needed to relax. I spent a lot of time in the bath these days, especially since I was always scared. I was probably the only person in New Dallas to still have a bath, and I revelled in the luxury of it. Lee had found it in an old compound they'd raided, and convinced a couple of privates to bring it back for me. It was the perfect present, and never as useful as it was right now. I could use the water to block out my fear, to keep myself staid until Lee came back. If she came back.

It was something I'd had to get used to over the years. I didn't get into this with my eyes closed. I met Lee exactly because she was in the emergency corps, and because her unit happened to be in the right place when my university complex gave in to the pressure of the surge. That hadn't been the only electricity I'd witnessed that night, either. She had made love to me in the wreckage of the science block, and as my hands had scraped down the strong skin of her back, we'd made a promise to stay together.

And so far, we'd kept it. I pulled myself up out of the bath water, pulling on an old towelling robe that I kept by the bath. I wandered out to the balcony to watch the unfolding chaos, startled by the pool of calm that lapped around my stomach. The streets below were tinged with the orange streaks of mass anger, and I wondered which of the figures I could see rushing underneath me would be the first to burn. I watched as a man rushed across the street to yell at a woman, and I knew I would never get to find out if they knew each other because, as he reached the sidewalk, a loud crash of lightning surged from within him. It was that easy to let your moods get the better of you.

The door flew open and I saw Lee standing in the middle of the large front room. As I ran to hold her, she grasped my hands and kept me at arm's length.

'Anita.' She said my name breathlessly. 'You have to listen to me. It's crazy out there, seriously. The EC's pulled out of patrolling. We're being left alone, do you understand?'

I let my breath out slowly. 'So it's true.'

Lee nodded slowly. Up until now, I hadn't quite believed it. I had assumed that Lee would come back and say it was a news hoax. There were underground theories that a large-scale mass panic would be enough to deal with all the excess energy, and there were plenty of groups prepared to try the plan out for size.

But this was no hoax. The world really was ending. Lee's grip relaxed on my hands and I pulled her into me, letting her frame fit solidly against mine. She was crying. The EC was a vocation to Lee, the only thing aside from me that made her life complete. She was certain that she could do some good that way. The injustice of enforced failure leaked from her limbs, and I wrapped her up in my arms.

'It's OK,' I whispered, and she nodded softly as I teased my lips against her neck, planting kisses soft enough to melt her tension. She leant towards me and I followed the trail of her shoulder, feeling her cool skin against my lips. She sighed, a sigh that said it was all over. I peeled away the rough khaki shirt slowly and her eyes widened. Not the time, not the place. What else was left to say?

Our bed was a large, heavy wooden thing, again a refugee of one of Lee's raided buildings. It was huge and sturdy, just like Lee. Just like us. Today, we needed to be more than ever. My hands still slipped beneath her shirt, resting on the taut breasts below, I pulled her over to it. Any resistance, any lingering sadness, flitted from her as I tweaked her nipples between my index fingers and thumbs. She landed on the bed at the first push on her chest.

Her skin smelt of dirt and sweat, and I breathed it in heavily as I lowered myself down to her, grazing my lips against her breast. Lee's skin is tough, hard, the seasoned skin of long tours of duty. It's one of the few constants I can count on these days: the unfailing firmness of her. I never realised that, despite her constancy, she would be how I spent my last minutes alive.

She sighed softly, her hand trailing casually through my hair as I traced a line of kisses down her stomach. Part of me was waiting for an explosion, for an eclipse. Her fatigues slid easily away as I followed the line of her hip bone, as my lips came to rest on her. She was already hot, and I rested my cheek against the inside of her thigh, sighing. I heard her moan slightly as I parted her, teasing the hot skin with my tongue. I explored her gently, hoping that, if this really was the last day I'd ever spend on Earth, I'd die savouring every inch of Lee's skin in my mouth. She gripped me with her thighs as I probed more deeply, feeling her shudder against me. As she came, she dug her nails into my shoulder and I took as big a breath of her as I could contain. This might be the last time I would ever be here.

Or, it could be, if I let it. Which I didn't. She was still running her hand through her hair to steady herself when I covered her mouth with mine, my lips searching, seeking,

132

desperate for an answer. My knee slipped between her thighs and I cupped each of her breasts with my hands. She was sweating, and I almost hoped that it would be enough to stick us together, for ever.

My hand slipped lower, grazing the strong, slender skin of her stomach. For a few moments, I simply kissed her, my palm resting on the mound of her like it was the most sacred place in the world. Then, I let my fingers wander. Slowly at first, simply testing, stroking slim lines along the inside of her. I wrote messages of love on her skin, hoping that she would somehow read them, but her lips were still resting against mine and sighing. I let my hand slip inside, let my thumb find the tiny knot of flesh I wanted. I pressed it carefully, forcefully, the rebound shaking through her firmly. She moaned, and nipped at my lip lightly. I smiled, my fingers working to a faster rhythm, her hips closing tightly around me. She shuddered as I moved, until she finally bucked against my hand, letting out the most beautiful note of a scream I had ever heard. I ran my hand through her now wet hair, and lowered my mouth down her body. Softly I planted a single kiss on her cunt, and rested my head there.

We stayed like that for what seemed like hours, the rivulets of sweat that had gathered on her thighs cooling against my face, her hand still resting on my shoulder. I couldn't bring myself to move away from her, couldn't stop myself from thinking that maybe we could end it all like this. Eventually, she brought herself slowly to crouch in front of me, her hands cupping my face. I thought, at first, that she was going to say something, that she wanted to be really sure I'd hear her. But she just looked at me, and I felt myself remember how I came to fall in love with her, how she used to look at me as if she'd never seen anything like me before.

'I don't want it to be over.' I almost didn't hear my own voice as I whispered it.

'Me neither.'

'How long do we have?' For a second, I wondered if I had lifted outside of myself, it seemed so surreal to be talking so calmly about this.

133

'I don't know. Maybe a couple of hours. Maybe a few days. It depends on how people take it, on whether or not the surge takes full hold. On how fast fires spread.' She shrugged.

'There was nothing else you could have done.'

Again she shrugged. Any other situation and I would have found this nonchalance reassuring.

'So ...' I started. I wasn't quite sure how to phrase this. 'What should we ... do?'

Lee arched a single eyebrow. I smiled. Of course. What other way to end the world?

If I had to count the times I'd wanted to die in a lover's arms, or the times I thought that my orgasm was too much for me that I would surely die of happiness, I could have harnessed all those moments into one stellar cyanide pill. Everything going pear shaped, sure that the end is nigh – well, slip this capsule onto your tongue and die tasting the pinks and reds and oranges of ecstasy. If only.

Outside, the sky tinged yellow. I built myself a den of duvet and slithered down Lee's body. I paused, wondering if I could count the hairs on her perfect cunt and burn it onto the innards of my brain. I paused too long, clearly, as she pinched me on the bottom to remind me she was waiting.

Inside she was hot and flowing, and I drank her in hungrily, clasping her firmly against my mouth. I licked firmly at her clit, feeling the fever burn through her body, hearing her moans growing lower, guttural. I smiled and let my tongue come to a perfect rest over her clit, relishing the sensation of her bucking and folding against me, the deliciousness of her orgasm against my lips. For all I cared, this could be the end right here.

She smiled at me, wickedly, and in one second flat flipped me over. There's another use for that strength of hers. Propped up on her elbows, she dipped down to kiss me, her nose grazing mine as she did so. She touched my lips fleetingly, before she moved to my ear, my neck, my shoulder. My breast. One nipple in her mouth, she teased it with her tongue, and I felt a delicious tug in my stomach. All this seemed enough to cause our own private electrocution.

Her tongue licked gently down past my navel, and I felt my hips rise in anticipation. Light as air, her tongue was inside me, the tiniest of movements against my skin, against my clit. I felt the first hint of a shake already, and she slowed, moving to my thighs to stall me. She kissed each inch of my leg, down to my toe then back again. My cunt felt as if it would burn if she didn't touch me soon.

But she did. Her tongue lapping furiously against my clit, I gripped the duvet between my fingers. I shuddered hard, rocked, bucked as if my hips would dislocate before I came. Lee clasped me to her, and I felt the rumbling tear through my whole body until I couldn't take it any more, until I came hard against her, her mouth still not moving from the flowing hot skin beneath it. Whispering, more from lack of breath than anything else, I pressed my lips to her ear. 'I love you.'

'I love you too.'

As we lay tangled, the noise from the street that rose up to greet us worsened. We looked at each other, each one seeking comfort from the screams that wafted from below. It was reaching fever pitch down there, and for once I didn't want her inside knowledge or the hard truth. I wanted the ignorance that comes from not having expectations. And there was the part of me, however small, that still believed all this was impossible, that the whole world couldn't seriously come crashing down around us.

The first time, I thought I was in heaven. I remembered how I had hidden in the store room, crouched against a box of new pipettes, praying that I would be safe here.

'Miss?'

Lee's voice had been gentle, commanding.

'We have to get you out of here.'

She had crouched down in front of me after I shook my head, my teeth gritting.

'What's your name?'

'Anita.'

She smiled. 'Pretty name. Pretty girl.'

I scoffed.

'I know.' She winked. 'Not exactly the right time, huh?'

But she was wrong. It was the perfect time. The exact moment I needed to escape. Not to escape the surges or the blackouts. To escape myself. I was meant to be working to find a way to stop it, to harness it, to control the surge somehow. I couldn't understand it. Sure, I had the highest grade point average in my graduating class, but I couldn't find a way to understand something that came from our own anger.

I could understand skin. And lips. And a woman who radiated a kindness dampened by years of surveying wreckage and death. So I didn't talk about why I was scared, or what was about to happen. Instead, I leant forward to take her head into my hands and kiss her. I was desperate, longing. I probed her with my need to forget. She was willing to let me. It was a good agreement.

The first sign of the fire we knew was from the sprinklers. They came on in our flat before we even realised the smoke – a constant since the morning's casualties – was actually rising. We hurried into clothes and through the door to the balcony, easing our way onto the fire escape and up on to the roof. It was Lee that started towards the roof first, and I didn't think to question as I followed her. On the flat edge of our apartment building, she pulled me close to her, and we looked over the edge at the debris.

The fires were everywhere. Below us, there were people, cars, houses all burning as if they were chip wood. Lee squeezed my hand as I looked, and I knew that this was what she had been seeing all morning – how she knew that it was all over.

'There's nothing to stop the surge?'

'No, baby,' she told me.

'Will we …?' I couldn't bear to finish my question.

Lee nodded.

And here was I thinking that maybe we could just sink into unconsciousness.

What I did was sink into the only thing I knew I could trust. I eased her onto the warming concrete, my hands sliding up the shirt she had so hastily dressed in. I kissed the soft spot between her breasts, licking at the sweat that had gathered there. She was sweet, familiar. I leant my body weight over her, relieved by the warmth of her skin against my groin. Nothing bad could happen now.

I let my hands explore her torso, counting the lines across her skin, the downy hairs that led towards her pussy. I kissed her, the inside of her thighs, delighting in the heat against my lips. My tongue slipped inside her and she groaned, her hands ruffling my hair. Against the moistness of her skin, I lapped at her, teasing out the familiar shaking, the old heat. I ran my hands over the sides of her buttocks, the hard flesh that came from years of heavy-duty training.

The screams from the street below mingled with Lee's as she bucked against my mouth. I pressed myself into her, desperate to keep the moment going, not to let it end. Not to let us end. As she lifted me by the shoulders to kiss me, I focused on her smile, remembering it for posterity.

I allowed myself only brief looks at the street below. Lee's arms around my shoulders, we watched. Beneath us, we could see other lovers, entwined like we were, as if the city had exploded into a final orgy of last chances. Mothers clasped their children to them, their eyes desperate, seeking a safe place, somewhere to hide them until it was all over.

On our balcony, a mouse slipped out of a corner, creeping towards the ledge. I wondered if animals were immune, if they would survive this. Maybe all the human cities and compounds would become new animal tribes, giving them their turn at fucking up a planet. Somehow, the idea of a city run by mice cheered me up, as if it was an old story from a children's anthology. As if there was still something to smile at.

They say your life flashes before your eyes, but all I could think of was a list of old lovers, categorising them in my head to keep myself from crying. I remembered the guy I had sucked off in high school to prove to the cheerleading squad I wasn't really a dyke; I remembered the rival cheer captain I fucked at a game between our two teams. They seemed like old movies now, snapshots of sex that didn't belong to me, that didn't fit with who I was any more. I didn't think of their names, just their base character: selfish, idiotic, easy lay. I took a gentle look to my right. True love. I buried my face into Lee's shoulder, our fingers still laced tightly together. I forced myself to listen to her breathing, to count the slow, steady beats. She rested her head against mine and there we stayed, folded into each other, close enough to probably be counted as one corpse if there was anyone left to find us.

The sky was gnarly, knotted with huge snaps of lightning, with pink flames that flew down to unsuspecting victims below. It tinged with green, acid, bile in its colour. I had never seen a sky so angry, so menacing. The sky would be the end of it.

I tried to blot out the growing orange glow behind my eyes and squeezed Lee's fingers, my heart knotted. Even though I knew that I was speaking into her chest I whispered, 'Thank goodness I found you.'

I dug my head into the tautness of her skin. And waited.

For the Good
by Alyssa Turner

Stacy had never been that girl: the kind of woman who does things merely for shock value. In her world, days began with wheat toast and egg whites joined by one cup of decaf, then a simple peck goodbye for Todd on his way to work. Every day was the same – whole wheat and not a whole lot of surprises.

Volunteering weekends at the community soup kitchen was another reliable event, though the only eventful part was the chance to spend a little time with her latest obsession. Not knitting or the scrapbooking kick she'd been on last year; this fixation was something ... different. Stacy was a good girl – a good wife, a good parishioner and an upstanding member of her small community. But for the life of her, she couldn't shake this nagging infatuation, no matter how salacious it was.

'Would you do me a favour and make sure I don't bust my ass on this ladder?' Myra asked, gesturing for her to add some stability at the base and stretching to fasten a paper turkey to the wall. Year-old tape flapped loosely from its debut in last year's Thanksgiving poverty outreach dinner. She raised her voice, mocking the rules of decorum. 'Wasn't Dan in charge of the decorations? Cheap bastard.'

Myra had a slender, petite frame and even appeared frail at first glance. It always surprised Stacy to hear the brash, off-colour remarks she dispensed on a regular basis. They became fast friends at the kitchen, but Stacy was careful not to carry their relationship out of the building; scared of what might happen if she dared to challenge happenstance. She simply didn't trust herself alone with this lover of women who made her wonder about undiscovered paths.

As Myra teetered on the ladder, Stacy found herself peering under her miniskirt, making out the round curve of her bottom. *What was it about her?* She didn't know, but the secret floated in the scent of the air when she passed, making Stacy want to take a deep breath.

Myra shifted to maintain her balance and Stacy got a good view of her silky panties, unexpectedly sheer, the soft rise of her lips beyond. She stared, and really didn't care to remember that someone might be watching. In the shadows, she could just make out the barest of skin scarcely sheathed from the rest of the world in fine black mesh. Stacy had thought about being completely bare – down there – but hadn't found the courage to go to the salon and have it done. A smile arrived with the idea of her and Myra going together.

Then Myra was losing her balance and Stacy reached to lend support, her hand reflexively slipping under her butt. In that instant, Stacy was awash with adrenaline and her hand lingered a moment longer than was appropriate.

Myra passed a slight smirk over her shoulder down to Stacy. 'I knew you'd come in handy. Thanks.'

Stacy yanked her hand away, tucking it quickly behind her back. 'I'm sorry.'

Thoughtfully, Myra let her tongue dance slowly over her teeth while her eyes burned into Stacy's skin, putting her further on the spot.

'Lunch.' The announcement from across the room delivered Stacy a welcome respite.

She cleared her throat. 'I'll grab you a sandwich. Grilled chicken, right?'

'Thanks, hon, I'll save you a seat.'

Stacy claimed two neatly wrapped paper bundles and slipped into the chair next to her, marvelling at how Myra tended to hold everyone captive with her gritty wit.

'I didn't go all the way to Queens just to hear about the price of milk. The painful thing about mothers is you never grow up enough to tell them to shut it.' Myra laughed casually as did Jake and Marci who shared the table and nodded with knowing agreement.

Neither of them would have guessed that underneath the table she had begun to trail her fingers up Stacy's leg. Myra dared her to put a stop to it. With each whisper of her fingers on her thigh she challenged Stacy to brush her away. Stacy did nothing. And when Myra suddenly grabbed her, the action merely produced a jolt and an exaggerated blurt of laughter with the intent to deter any suspicion.

Myra smiled directly at her and continued. 'You know it's like I spent my entire childhood listening to her tell me to be quiet and the only way I can escape hearing about my cousin's new McMansion is to fake a call waiting on the other line.' Those fingers slowed again on Stacy's thigh, circling and stroking, squeezing ever so slightly.

Stacy looked around, her heart thundering inside her neat cashmere sweater. It was dizzying – the audacity, the sheer naughtiness. But Stacy's silent invitation hollered for more with her passive acquiescence.

When Myra's hand climbed all the way up, to the nest of warmth between her thighs, Stacy only closed her eyes and rested her head on her index finger. The image paraded in the darkness, Myra's fingers tracing the edges of her sensible cotton briefs through her leggings. Then a pinkie presented itself, small and skilled on her bud, circling and dabbing so very softly, barely detectable, but growing more present with every passing minute. All the while, Myra continued to chat and eat, as if nothing were happening at all.

'Stacy, are you all right?' Jake asked, noticing she had become quiet; her eyes still closed with a distant expression on her face. He had to ask twice, calling, 'Stacy, did you hear me,' and finally bringing her back to the conversation.

'I'm fine,' she said, but excused herself nonetheless. In truth, Stacy had become uncomfortably wet inside her panties and needed to escape to the bathroom.

Her thoughts were racing, thrashing about in her head. She couldn't ask her, could not even look over her shoulder with a silent plea. Stacy was only able to pray that she would follow.

Not long after Stacy closed the door to her stall, she heard

Myra's motorcycle boots clacking on the tile floor.

'Where are yooooouuu?' she called playfully, pushing open each stall door until she reached a locked one. 'Do you want me to come in there?'

Softly, in spite of herself, Stacy whispered, 'Yes,' and unlocked the door.

With a flick of her wrist, Myra gave a push and it creaked open to reveal Stacy's leggings were already down at her ankles. She paused a moment before stepping in and securing the door behind her.

'How much do you want this?' Myra challenged, forcing Stacy to spell out her desire.

'A lot,' she puffed as if the words were forced from her lips.

Myra boldly placed her hand onto Stacy's sopping vagina. 'Mmm. Yes, I see,' she purred, running her fingers through the slippery creases.

Stacy was startled. 'Oh!' And startled again by the rattling stall as she staggered to the side.

Myra inched nearer, her other hand disappearing into the brown sea of Stacy's hair. 'I promise, I don't bite.'

The back of her head slipped easily into the cup of Myra's small palm and Stacy found little resistance in her neck as Myra drew her mouth to hers. In the roundness of her tongue, Stacy relived the smoky haze of a girl who had never been kissed – that is never been kissed, by a girl.

That tongue, so patient at first, was drawing on Stacy's rising desire and feeding it slowly with unrelenting persistence. On and deeper into the soft wetness she probed – a sweet prelude and treated as such. When Myra chose to suck gently on her neck and twist her ripe nipple softly between two fingers, the result was more combustible than she expected.

Stacy stumbled again.

'Let me help you with those,' Myra proposed, gesturing to the jumble of blended lycra catching her ankles.

Stacy offered up one leg and then the other. No longer trapped, Myra directed her to stand on the toilet. The cold metal stall provided a reliable support under her white-knuckle grip as Myra raised one of her thighs and delicately introduced her tongue into the heat of Stacy's core.

'Ooh … my …' Stacy simply couldn't wrap her mind around the feeling, but she was melting in the delight of it despite the chill of the recycled air.

Sure, her husband made a habit of treating her to some oral attention on the regular, but never had the sensation been quite like what Myra elicited with a spectacular ensemble of dips, twists and swirls. Her eyes rolled back as Myra's tongue swept to and fro with just the right amount of firmness and a rhythm meant to keep a gasp poised in Stacy's throat.

With eyes closed, her hand found Myra's head and drew her closer, needful for every pass more than the last. Stacy marvelled at the delicious sounds escaping that petite mouth as Myra drank her in and occasionally glanced up to spy her pleasured expression. A sway of her hips, dragging, now stop and then again – Stacy gratuitously rocked over Myra's open mouth, letting the feeling rule her entirely.

Myra was making her gulp for air, thinking that she might just hyperventilate and pass out. She held on tight to the steel wall meant for privacy, but not so good at containing her rising moans. The slipping, the sliding, the sipping and tugging were making her delirious with lust and she began to imagine what it would be like to return the favour. Stacy visualised every sweep and lick round her clit and into her crevice. She saw herself doing the same and the image cooked up a new batch of elixir for Myra to lap at.

'Come for me, baby.' Myra cooed, in the time it took to dip two fingers deep inside her. Then with nary a beat skipped, it was more of the same genius manoeuvres from her hot mouth.

'Oh God!' The words were shivering on her lips yet hazardously loud despite the nagging reminder of their semi-private surroundings.

Still Myra wanted more and knew exactly how to get it, rolling her fingers slightly on entry and withdrawing with the upturn of her tongue. That solicited another outburst – music to her ears.

'How long?'

Stacy managed an inquisitive grunt.

143

'How long have you wanted this?' Myra asked, seizing another opportunity to make her claim.

'Really long.'

'Not as long as me,' she purred and ran her fingers into Stacy's cunt with the speed of intention. Stacy's knees buckled and Myra worked her licks into overdrive.

It wasn't long any more. With a proper climax breaking free against Myra's busy tongue, a raw and fierce hunger flooded her every recess. Gripped by it, Stacy poured herself out entirely until she was a mass of quivering nerves.

But in the afterglow, she needed help. *Yes, yes ... help. I need help, because I don't know what I'm doing and I can't feel my legs.* The look of desperation on Stacy's face even startled Myra, who then produced a hand, delicate in the air and held patiently still until Stacy reached for it with trembling fingers.

On Myra's assistance, Stacy climbed down from her perch and received a sweet kiss once grounded. The taste of her own juices left sticky on Myra's mouth made Stacy even more impatient to know her unique flavour. Myra drew her closer, wrapping her arms around her neck possessively. But Stacy resisted, instead guiding Myra to take her previous position on top of the basin.

Follow my instinct, that's all I have to do.

Myra pulled up her skirt, and Stacy yanked down her panties to reveal plumped lips eager to be caressed in return.

Stacy had always appreciated the female form, but until now settled only for the offerings of her own. In the morning after Todd left for work, she regularly revelled in the feel of herself. Luxuriating in the velvety softness that is woman, she'd float her fingers over the curves rising from the landscape of her body. Myra, up close, was far more captivating.

She took it slow, celebrating the moment with tentative strokes of her fingers on Myra's responsive lips. Stacy watched in amazement as each touch produced a quiver and a sigh. A single finger pressed into her wetness and retracted produced a string of silk for curious inspection.

And then a taste.

Gently, Stacy extended her tongue onto the tip of Myra's clit, barely – softly – tasting.

The ginger sweeps she delivered sent Myra's breathing into low rough growls, crying out every time Stacy's tongue slipped over her. Myra was sweeter than Stacy could have imagined and she absolutely delighted in the way Myra's fingertips played in her hair, encouraging her to continue.

Stacy grew more confident and drove her face into Myra's glistening pussy.

'Yes, that's right. Have me.'

Have her. I can – I am ... having her. No more wanting, wondering. No more thinking, just doing. And Stacy went with her instinct and had as much of Myra as she could. She plundered her, gulping and slurping feverishly with a watering mouth and pursed lips. Hungry for the taste of her, she persisted and learnt quickly what details were most appreciated.

Myra offered her gratitude for the freshman effort with a bath of renewed slickness for Stacy's chin.

'Oh fuck, Stacy. You're going to make me come.' Myra sounded surprised her orgasm was ushered in so quickly. It was just as much of a shock to Stacy that she delivered such an irresistible reason. And if she could bring her to the edge, then she could back her away and enjoy her rise all over again.

She slowed. Each lick now languished lightly on the surface of her, dancing with the tune of soft whimpers falling from Myra's open mouth.

'You bitch, you're teasing me.'

Stacy grinned but her tongue remained on task. Myra grinned too, and focused on the flurrying caresses dismantling her. The more she forced her hips forward, the less she received from Stacy, until she couldn't tell if she was only imagining the tickles of breath making her want to scream. Myra wasn't used to feeling like this, so open. And in the end, that was more arousing than anything else.

She shuddered and contracted. The promise of Stacy's mouth on her again haunted her senses and her need for its return was incorrigible. It was no matter that Stacy barely touched her now; Myra was careening over the edge after all and coming with a vengeance down her thighs.

That did it. Myra's grunts proceeded into chuckles – incredulous about the entire event. Stacy began to laugh too, completely astounded by what she had just done.

'Hon, you made my day.'

Stacy only smiled. 'Let's get back out there. We still have work to do.'

The lunch crowd had broken up and the two picked up where they left off with the decorations, feeling very much in the giving spirit.

As far as Todd was concerned, community service remained an important part of Stacy's life. And as in the past, her visits to the soup kitchen continued to be rewarding … in more ways than one.

The Perfect Italian Wife
by Toni Sands

The ocean shimmered luminous green behind Vicenzo as he talked on the phone to London or Paris – or maybe Madrid. Melissa had been instantly attracted when, as cabin crew, she welcomed the tycoon to the Boeing 747's upper-class suite. Three years later he could still ignite her with a look. The heir to the Trapani hotel empire fixed those melting toffee eyes on her and closed out his conversation.

'I go to London on Monday, Melissa. Will you accompany me? I need to travel to Edinburgh too. And Paris after that.'

She knew hordes of women would barrel down Niagara Falls to life-swap with her. But this time she didn't want to stay in the Knightsbridge Trapani, despite its classy boutique and restful spa. Even though she hated parting from him, Melissa had a plan. She watched his eyes devour her cleavage. Her hands were already loosening the oyster satin peignoir. Still his question hung in the air.

Slinky as a cat, Melissa rose and knelt before him, holding his gaze while she unfastened his robe. She buried her head in his lap. Vicenzo gripped her silver-blonde tresses with both hands, sucking in his breath as his cock sprang to life. Melissa's mouth was heaven. And at this rate he was going there. Fast. Gently he stopped her. Dragged her onto his lap. Gasped as she captured him inside her cunt and rode him to ecstasy. Their fantastic fast fuck led to their fast return to bed.

'I hope I haven't made you horribly late,' she said an hour later, watching him button his pink Jermyn Street shirt.

'So, will you come with me next week?'

'I know you're longing for an heir, my darling.' She watched him strap on the Cartier watch she'd chosen for his 40th birthday. 'And soon I'll be busy furnishing our new home. I'd like to arrange a reunion with my bridesmaids before things get hectic.'

'So invite them! They can stay here. Or take them cruising. Papa's still in Florida. He won't need the yacht. I'll speak to Karl.'

'Vicenzo, that's perfect. A girly cruise. Won't Captain Karl just love that?'

'And won't I just miss you, my beautiful wife.' Regret clouded his eyes.

But Melissa resisted. They planned to move into a villa instead of luxuriating in the hotel's penthouse suite. The prospect of a break with her friends excited her. Vicenzo's engagingly camp yacht master knew every exclusive mooring on the Amalfi coast – and then some. The silk handkerchief she selected for her husband exactly matched his shirt. And as she tucked the square into his top pocket she caught a drift of his cologne. It transported her to a lemon grove on a dewy morning with sunshine melting the mist. Just like the first time he'd fucked her.

She'd be wet again if she didn't shoo him to his office. 'Think about our own reunion afterwards,' she said. 'I'll be so hot for you; you'll need to keep the next morning free.' She watched his face. 'But now, I need to contact the girls.'

'Three gorgeous girls together – you better be good,' Vicenzo called over his shoulder on his way out.

Oh, we will be, thought Melissa, heading for the Gaggia and some fresh coffee. If her friends could join her, she'd make sure this holiday remained in their memories for a very long time. Surely Riley and Joy would understand her need to escape her gilded cage? Afterwards, she'd settle down and be a good Italian wife.

Joy gazed round the sumptuous salon of the *MV Passione*. 'I can't believe this. A whole week of luxury without husband or kids.' She smiled dreamily as the steward offered her a glass of champagne.

'I'm so lucky you could both make it.' Melissa crossed her legs and sank into white velvet cushions.

'It's cost me some long-haul trips,' said Riley, folding her slender limbs beneath her. 'But it's worth it to see you two.'

'Do you miss your old life, Melissa? Seeing Riley and being reminded of it all?'

Riley laughed. 'Joy, sweetie, what are you saying? She's traded in rosters and recycled air for – oh, I'm so jealous. Mr Sex on Legs or what …?'

'OK, guys,' Melissa said. 'Here's to a fabulous holiday.' They clinked glasses.

'So what's the plan?' Riley leant forward.

'Do we need a plan?' Joy's gaze lingered on Luigi's tight buns as he retrieved a fallen serviette.

Melissa was amused. This was promising. 'I'll explain more over dinner.'

Riley was reading the menu. 'I'll never fit back into my uniform unless I take some exercise this week. You'd better push me into that mini gym.'

Her hostess's lips twitched. 'Hopefully you'll get a satisfactory workout. As well as have fun.'

After dinner, Luigi served espressos and brandy and left them alone.

'Don't say you want to go moonlight skinny-dipping?' Riley rolled her brown eyes.

'I was wondering about the pirate life. I've always wanted to get into role play. This is the perfect opportunity.'

Silence. 'Are you serious?' Joy sat up straight.

'Absolutely,' said Melissa. 'I'd never be unfaithful to my darling Vicenzo but I'd love to tumble some boundaries.'

'Hello,' Riley drawled. 'Isn't piracy illegal? And surely you've got enough treasure, honey-bun?'

'We won't break any laws, though we might bend them. We're going to dress up as pirates. But, when we board another vessel, it won't be jewels or cash we're after. Excuse me for one moment.'

Melissa left the saloon. There was telltale dampness between her thighs and she hoped the others would feel that same frisson once they learnt what lay ahead.

She returned, carrying a Gucci holdall in one hand and a silver hatbox in the other. She placed them beside her chair then closed the door behind her, turning the key in the lock before unzipping the bag. Her breasts rose and fell, showcasing her excitement. She pulled out a costume and held it in front of her. The long-sleeved hot pink jacket was piped with gold braiding. It fastened corset-style, its ties also gold. Underneath, a froth of white lace topped a pale pink mini dress. From a cloud of tissue paper Melissa produced a fuchsia-pink pirate hat crowned with black plumage.

'You like?' she said. 'You'd better be the same size as you were on my wedding day. But no pastel satin pumps this time. Wait till you see the kinky boots in my cabin. And I've chosen other goodies to, um, spice things up.'

Riley whistled. Joy's face was a mix of longing and apprehension.

'Let's look at the other outfits,' Melissa said. 'Then decide who gets first pick of the accessories.'

When they cracked open another bottle to celebrate the alliance of the pirate wenches, Joy was dressed in the pink outfit. Melissa wore a similar one in dramatic purple. Redhead Riley wore a leather mini dress with handkerchief point hem. The deep plunge front showed off her perfect creamy breasts. Melissa had decided Riley had the balls to carry off the outfit and was proved right. All three wore suede boots with leather straps and silver buckles. Stockings or tights were suitably saucy.

'These little skull and crossbones motifs are cute,' said Joy, inspecting her legs. 'But what do we actually do if we board a strange yacht?'

'Indulge our fantasies,' said Melissa. 'I've always wanted to perform.' She took another sip of bubbly. 'You know – dress up and act out of character. Joy, darling, don't look so worried.'

Joy's smile was wobbly. 'I don't know if I can,' she said.

'Make a spectacle of myself, I mean.'

Riley patted her hand. 'Who's to know? Who's going to recognise Joy Bennett, teacher from Twickenham? You'll be transformed by that wig. What a turn-on!'

'Let me get this straight,' said Joy. 'Tomorrow we moor at San Terrano. The crew get the night off. We dress up and find a yacht with only men on board? Just like that?'

'We'll do our homework,' said Melissa. 'After our siesta, we'll browse the marina and the shops and follow any likely victims.'

Riley giggled. 'And you a respectable married woman.'

'Don't get me wrong,' said Melissa. 'I love Vicenzo. I don't intend cheating on him. But it's time I accepted my responsibilities.' She had their full attention. 'If I don't get to indulge my fantasies first, I'll always … regret it.'

'Fantasies?' Riley was playing with her hair.

Melissa pulled the Gucci holdall towards her. She delved inside and produced a pair of gilded handcuffs. Then some leather restraints – butch with metal buckles. She hesitated before displaying the next object. 'A cat o'nine tails, in case you're not familiar.'

'Looks like we soon will be,' Riley whispered. 'You're playing a dangerous game, my friend.'

'I know,' said Melissa.

The following afternoon the women strolled round San Terrano in the sunshine. At a café with a yellow awning, Riley ordered drinks. One or two pairs of men settled at neighbouring tables. The women exchanged glances. These guys had to be gay. Then Riley's elbow jabbed Joy in the ribs. 'Look – leaving that delicatessen. I bet they're straight.'

Two tall men in shorts, T-shirts and flip-flops were in deep conversation. They glanced across the square at the stunning trio then began walking towards the café.

'Piece of panettone,' murmured Riley as the two guys chose a nearby table. Immediately, two blondes with endless legs and waterfall hair appeared from nowhere and joined the men.

'Looks like a quiet night in with the girls,' said Melissa with a sigh.

Before dinner that evening, Joy suggested they dress up anyway but the others shouted her down. 'The crew mustn't know,' warned Melissa. 'Tomorrow we sail to Marina d'America for two nights. You'll love it. And I think we'll score.'

They toasted one another. But Melissa suspected each of them was fantasising about what might happen if things went their way. So, she'd hidden a personal vibrator inside a honey-coloured teddy bear, beneath their pillows, to ensure they slept sweetly. Her own sexual appetite was so heightened that she longed for bedtime.

Alone in the master suite, she climbed into bed naked. And rang Vicenzo. 'Talk to me, baby,' she said. 'Already I miss you.'

He began murmuring in Italian. The hot dirty words she needed. She placed her vibrator between her thighs, her mind trawling her fantasy of being fucked by a stranger. With each stroke and spasm she climbed closer to the edge. And when she melted into oblivion she muffled her cry against the teddy bear.

'It should be me inside your sweet, sticky cunt.' Vicenzo's voice was melted chocolate down the phone.

'Soon, baby. Soon.'

Marina d'America snoozed in the sunshine as the *MV Passione* snuck into her berth next day. After a lazy lunch, Melissa requested a cold supper for later and instructed Captain Karl and his crew to take the evening off. It was time to do some homework. She knew her friends enjoyed browsing boutiques and, as they left the yacht, Melissa wondered if the others were as hungry as she was for a new experience.

But as they strolled along the quayside, sharp-eyed Riley noticed the Union Jack fluttering nearby. Two guys were lounging on the sun deck of a luxury yacht about six berths away. Both men sat upright as the women approached.

'Good afternoon, ladies,' called one.

'Going far?' His friend asked.

'Where would you recommend?' Riley made the challenge.

'Nowhere better than here,' said the first guy. 'We have lager, white wine or iced tea.'

'Well,' Riley pretended to consult the others. 'Seeing as there's safety in numbers ...'

An hour later, the women left Marcus and Toby and walked back to their own yacht. Even Riley had said shopping could wait. Back on board, she hugged each of her two friends in turn. 'Can you believe our luck? A stag cruise! Groom, best man and another two guys due later.'

'It's perfect,' said Melissa. 'Definitely no strings. Drinks on board at seven. We're going to be quite a surprise for the two we haven't met.'

'We'll be quite a surprise for all of them,' said Joy primly. 'Especially when they see Riley in that slashed top.'

'Are we all quite sure we're up for it?' Melissa searched their faces. 'You know the rules. We don't have sex with them. We lure them into submission. We dominate them. We torment them. Don't wimp out, Joy.'

'You know you want to dress up, Joy. We'll look after you.' Riley looked sly. 'But what if we really fancy one of them? And he feels the same. Can't we ... you know?'

'Two of us have husbands,' Melissa protested.

Joy looked thoughtful.

After supper the transformation took place. Melissa's blonde tresses were hidden beneath a boyish mop of copper curls. Joy was now a raven-haired stunner. And Riley's sleek red bob was transformed into a golden tangle.

'Are you wearing your pirate panties underneath? In case you want to tease your captives with a little, shall we say, intimate description,' Melissa added.

'Like telephone sex?' Riley hitched up her brief skirt to display a black eye patch garter. Its sequins glittered against her cobweb stockings.

'A glass of champagne to set the mood?' Melissa shivered at the thought of what the night might bring. How far were she and her friends really prepared to go?

Two glasses later, the wenches set off, each carrying a satchel. There was no sign of their hosts as they reached their destination. Within moments, Melissa had boarded. She held out her hand to Riley. Joy hesitated. Then she too grabbed at Melissa.

'I hear voices,' she said. 'Come on – before I change my mind.'

When the three sexy pirates burst in, Marcus jumped to his feet. Bridegroom Toby stopped sprawling on the window seat. The men exchanged glances.

'You ladies are full of surprises.' Marcus's gaze centred on Melissa's breasts straining her laces.

'Where's the rest of your crew?' Her voice was brusque.

'Delayed in Paris, poor sods. Rail strike,' Toby drawled. 'You'll have to make do with the two of us.'

Melissa nodded at Riley. 'Cuff him,' she hissed. 'For insubordination.'

Riley stepped forward. She delved into her leather satchel and withdrew a pair of silky black rope restraints. Toby looked startled. He glanced at Marcus.

'He can't help you,' Riley snapped, grabbing Toby's wrist.

Joy dealt with his other one. She glanced down at his impressive erection and sucked in her breath. Swiftly she knelt and began binding Toby's ankles with silver bondage tape. 'He's loving it,' she crooned.

Marcus's laughter faded as Riley and Melissa advanced. He backed away, stumbled and collapsed in an armchair. Melissa had his hands manacled by the time Joy moved in with her scary tape. Melissa shrugged off her jacket.

She moved closer to Marcus, thrusting her perfumed breasts towards his face. 'Don't you have a drink for a thirsty wench? Oh, but you can't move, can you? Foolish me.'

'We'll just have to help ourselves, won't we?' Riley stood, legs apart, her tight skirt straining over her lovely arse. Her cheeks were flushed. Her breathing was jagged. She went over to the ice bucket and expertly popped a cork. The invasion had begun. As she watched Riley pour Dom Perignon into flutes, Melissa knew Marcus was watching her. She felt empowered.

And her scanty pirate panties were damp.

Riley sashayed over to Toby and held her glass so he could sip. She put the drink down and lowered herself onto his lap, wriggling into place. 'My, he's hard,' she said. She stood, turned round and sat astride him this time, rubbing her crotch against his erection. 'Nice,' she sighed. 'Should I continue, Mistress?'

Melissa yelled, 'No, impudent wench!' She produced a cat o'nine tails which she held before her and swished a couple of times. As she eyed Riley's taut behind, Riley got off Toby's lap. He was silent but Melissa saw him gulp. And lick his lips. 'Bend over,' she said, caramel soft. She swished the cat again. Its red leather tails ended in miniature skulls. Melissa stepped forward and put her mouth to Riley's ear. 'Ready, hon?'

One imperceptible nod was enough. As Riley bent over, hands grasping Toby's knees for support, Melissa exposed her friend's bottom. There was a gap of creamy flesh between Riley's black lace thong and her cobweb stockings. Melissa raised the cat. It swooshed through the air and lightly whipped the pert cheeks of Riley's arse. Melissa's second swish was less gentle. But when she trickled the thongs across the other wench's rump, Riley tensed her bum and whimpered.

'More?' Melissa purred.

Riley nodded. This time, as the tails bit, she gasped. 'Do it again, Mistress!' Raising her arm, Melissa obeyed. The tails sliced the air and splayed across Riley's bum cheeks. Again Melissa flicked the fronds gently backwards and forwards.

Riley rocked herself. 'I'm almost there,' she shrieked.

'Shall we help her relieve her agony?' Melissa didn't wait for an answer.

The guys were transfixed. Joy gulped at her champagne. Her cheeks were flushed. Riley was sobbing. Melissa handed her a dildo. Riley knelt on the floor, panting and writhing as she coaxed herself to orgasm in front of four people. As she watched the storm subside, Melissa's hands were trembling.

'How much can a man take?' Marcus's hoarse voice broke the spell.

Joy came forward. 'Shall we find out?'

Melissa whirled around. 'You're very bold, Missy. D'you fancy a taste of the cat too?' Her eyes glittered.

Joy stood her ground. 'Only if you release this pretty gentleman's hands. I want him to chastise me.'

This lifted role play beyond Melissa's wildest dreams. 'Release him.' She nodded to Riley.

Marcus took the cat o'nine from Melissa, who pulled forward a leather stool. Joy stretched across it. Marcus pulled up her skirt. There was a sharp intake of breath as he saw the outline of her bottom beneath her flimsy knickers. Joy took four strokes of the cat. She gasped after each one. As his excitement mounted, Marcus's cock strained to escape his shorts. Melissa glanced round and saw Riley and Toby looking as aroused as the other two. Things happened quickly then. As Marcus paused with the cat held aloft, Joy twisted herself upright. She pulled off her panties and let them fall to the floor. She wriggled, leaning backwards, legs apart, hands gripping the sides of the stool, revealing her shaven pussy. She looked up at Marcus. He dropped the cat. And got to his knees, ankles still bound. Bending his head, he went down on Joy, moving like a man in a dream.

'Faster,' whispered Joy. And again. She buried her fingers in his hair, clinging to him. 'More …' She arched her back and climaxed, stretching her lovely throat as her body vibrated with pleasure. Her scream shattered the silence.

It was then Melissa knew she was on borrowed time. She picked up the cat o'nine tails, walked over to Toby and laid it beside him. She released his bonds. Then she stretched herself face down across him, so that her centre rested on his hard-on. Toby picked up the cat.

'Punish me,' begged Melissa.

'You deserve it,' he barked. 'You've led the other wenches into disrepute. And for that you must be whipped till you come. But first … first I'm going to pull down your frilly white knickers.'

Melissa lost all sense of time. She forgot she had an audience. She heard the tails whistle through the air. She felt the delicious hot sting on her bare flesh. And she groaned.

With each stroke she groaned louder. She shuddered each time, feeling Toby's erection judder against her clitoris. The next explosion of pleasure and pain made her cry out. Toby flung down the cat and cradled her as spasms overwhelmed her. No one moved. Then he whispered in Melissa's ear. 'What next, Mistress?

Back at the yacht, Melissa stripped and went straight to her shower. Dripping, she wrapped herself in a fluffy white towel. There was a tap on the door. Melissa let in her slightly dishevelled pirate friends.

'We couldn't just leave them like that,' said Riley.

'Was it good?' Melissa asked.

'Good enough,' said Joy. 'We were careful. But we wanted to get back to you. We had a little chat and we thought we should go for one more boundary push.'

Melissa looked from one to the other.

'On the bed,' said Riley. 'You know you want to.'

Melissa's mouth dried. 'Oh, wow ...' she said. But she moved across to the big divan, letting her towel fall to the floor. The other two removed their costumes. Melissa watched, her eyes widening at the sight of Riley's high rounded breasts and boyish hips. Joy's curves were lush and billowing by comparison. The women lay either side of Melissa.

Riley had brought three velvet masks to bed. 'While we wear these, we're off limits,' she said.

Melissa put on her mask. She reached for Joy and began running her hands across her friend's breasts. She bent and began licking the nipples. Joy lay back.

Riley gently parted Joy's legs. 'I'll stroke you very, very lightly while Melissa sucks you.'

Joy's breathing became more rapid. Soon she was telling them what she wanted them to do next. What she liked most ... faster, slower ... until her orgasm lifted her up and away. She opened her eyes and smiled up at them. 'May I watch you two now? It's something I've always fantasised about.' She wriggled away and curled up at the foot of the bed.

Melissa reached for some lube. 'Lie back,' she said.

Riley obeyed. Melissa kissed her friend on the lips lightly at first, then passionately. Riley reached for Melissa's pert breasts, cupping and squeezing them till Melissa broke free and took some of the gel, smoothing it between Riley's thighs. With butterfly fingers she caressed her friend's body, lulling her, soothing her, tantalising her, until Riley's eyes glittered behind her mask. As her breathing became raucous, Melissa grabbed a dildo and placed it in her friend's hand. Riley was arching her back. 'Do it for me,' she begged.

Melissa heard Joy's sharp intake of breath. She nudged the dildo inside Riley's pussy lips, gently penetrating – pushing then pulling back. Her rhythm increased in confidence as she watched Riley's face. She saw her timing was right. With every gasp, Riley got closer. Her face contorted as she shared her most intimate moment with her closest friends.

When Joy joined them again, Melissa was at high doh. Even as Joy tentatively fingered her friend's nipples, Melissa shuddered with pleasure. 'I can do multiples,' she confessed.

Riley took charge. 'If you play with your nipples and Joy strokes lube round your frills, I'll tease your bottom.'

Melissa swallowed hard. Then lay on her side. She began rolling her nipples between her fingers. 'Nice and slow, Joy,' she murmured. 'Yes, just like that.' She squeezed her thighs together as the dildo teased her from behind. Up and down and around it went, until Melissa was so aroused that she begged, 'Push it in a little. Yes! Now, Joy. Fuck me faster.'

Five minutes later, the three were sprawled on the soft white bedding. Melissa doubted this would ever be repeated. The last few hours had surpassed even her wildest dreams.

After the others went to their cabins, there was something important left to do.

'My angel?'

'I've been a naughty girl,' she whispered into the mouthpiece.

'Tell.'

'The three of us dressed up as pirate wenches tonight. Afterwards, we got into bed together.'

There was a pause. Vicenzo said, 'And?'

'I … I liked it.'

He groaned into the phone. 'How I wish I could have watched you.'

She made a kissing sound. 'But you shall, my darling. I kept the camera running.'

'Melissa, my angel,' he said. 'You are the perfect Italian wife.'

Those Good Times
by Jennie Treverton

In all my straight life I'd never had such an unexpected jolt to
my snatch as I had on the day that Aia told me, gazing right
into my eyes, that she'd thought of me while she wanked. It
was while we were on our break, having a cigarette under the
corrugated awning in the backyard, a space we shared with the
seafood freezer and the dessert freezer and a bucket where
chefs' whites lay soaking in bleach. The smell of bleach fumes
are what I remember, in my mouth and eyes as much as my
nostrils, coating the back of my throat, making me blink, a
thick wall of it. Muffled clinks and chatter coming from the
restaurant. And Aia's bad black eyes looking into mine. I
always thought of her eyes as characteristically Eastern
European, for no other reason than they were dark, and
darkness made me think of mysticism, and the East, and
everything that I imagined Aia to come from, everything
opposite to me.

The way she said the word "wank" was cute. The end of the
word was clipped in the Essex style, not the kind of sub-Bond
girl "vaank" you'd expect from a girl from Bulgaria. Her grasp
of English was extraordinary. She'd lived here less than two
years. And that was almost all I knew about her, except what
I'd observed during work time. She ate slices of onion bread
when the chef wasn't looking. She took as many cigarette
breaks as she could possibly get away with. She couldn't cut a
butter-curl to save her life, but she had a way with the
customers and was good at convincing them to have dessert.

'So, yeah,' she said, 'but you don't mind, do you? You

don't mind that I told you.'

I smiled, thinking. Aia having a wank. How did she do it to herself? I remembered reading somewhere that for many women's whole lives, they use the same method for masturbating that they develop when they're young. There is an astonishing variety of styles, the vulva being such a neat and versatile thing. Women lie on their backs, on their fronts. They watch themselves in the mirror. They rub themselves up against pillows, chair legs, handfuls of duvet. They raid the kitchen for vegetables, they raid the bathroom for bottles.

What did Aia like to do?

'Aia,' I said, tapping my cigarette ash, 'there's so much I want to ask you, I don't know where to begin.'

She laughed quietly.

'I'm sure you can find somewhere to begin,' she said.

'I honestly had no idea.'

'Why would you?'

'I didn't even know you were gay.'

'I'm not gay. I love men, God, I love men and their cocks.' She laughed at how this sounded. 'Don't get me wrong.'

'But don't put you in a pigeonhole either,' I offered.

'That's right.'

'Don't shut yourself off to new experiences.'

'Exactly,' she said, looking up at me again. She was so much smaller than me – five foot nothing, if that. Her thick black fringe shone faintly green in the halogen floodlight. She had a ballpoint pen sticking diagonally into her ponytail. The look in her eyes went straight to my clit, and suddenly it was obvious. All those stupid adolescent clichés about good times and new experiences. The most stupid of them were the most true.

'So, you want to begin where?' she said.

'Tell me what you thought about just before you came,' I said, surprising myself.

'Oh, that,' she said, rolling her eyes and smiling broadly. 'Honey, you should have seen what you were doing. You were lying on my bed, and your clothes were all over the floor. Your knickers were on the pillow next to you. You were playing with yourself and begging me, *begging me* to come over and touch you. So this is the picture in my head. You directing me between your legs and showing me your cunt which is all wet and big. You're so excited and so desperate for me to touch you.'

She paused and took a drag on her cigarette.

'And then I crawled over the bed towards you. But I didn't touch you between your legs. I crawled up your body instead and I put my boob into your mouth. And that drove you wild. You were biting me and sucking, and I wanted to feel that mouth on me for real, God, I wanted it so, so bad. So what I did was this. I kept that picture of you in my head while I wanked my cunt with one hand and with my other hand I brought my boob up to my mouth and you know what? I can *just* reach it with my tongue. And as soon as I did that I came. Thinking about you.'

I didn't say anything.

'It wasn't much of a substitute, though. The very tip of my own tongue. It's not like what you were doing to me.'

I could feel the night air freezing the back of my throat. I closed my mouth.

'So,' she said, businesslike. 'What else do you want to know?'

I wanted to know why she'd decided to tell me this. Being a confessional type myself – can you tell? – I'm highly aware of other people's weaknesses for self-revelation. And Aia didn't give herself away lightly, I was sure of that, or else I'd have known a lot more about her than I did after God knows how many fag breaks on how many Saturday nights. She wasn't drunk either, that much was obvious. Which meant, I supposed, that she was making a deliberate move. On me.

She was very self-contained, very cool. Not looking at me now. No sideways glances as she blew her smoke into the night. Apparently it was my turn.

I threw my cigarette end down and faced her. The halogen had lit up all the tiny fine wisps around her hairline. In all my straight life I'd never seen such a thing as Aia.

The kitchen door swung open and slammed noisily into the

163

wall.

'Service, hussies,' said the chef.

And it was two full hours before I got to talk to her again. Ferrying platefuls, taking orders, I had time to plan a little. Here and there I glimpsed her as she carried a tray of coffees, pretended to laugh at something a customer said, picked up a dropped fork. She had a really beautiful arse. When she bent over, everybody looked. I marvelled that I'd never noticed before, this wave of silent attention she created when she moved. Accidentally I caught the eyes of one man who'd been looking at her. He looked guilty at first, then amused, slightly accusatory, obviously thinking I was jealous.

Perhaps, under normal circumstances, I might have been jealous. I could recognise that pattern of thought as mine, on an ordinary day. But at that moment envy was the furthest thing from my mind. She was interesting to me. She never stopped moving.

The next time I bumped into her was at the bar when we were both waiting for drinks orders.

She smiled coolly and said, 'Busy busy.'

'I've got another question for you,' I said.

'Oh yeah?'

'Yeah,' I said, looking at her hard.

She laughed and said, 'Not here though, right?'

'Best not.'

Her wine bucket was ready and she had to go. When she brushed past me I just caught her humming to herself.

From then on I was her stalker for the night. I was on her, and she knew it, while she swung her ponytail and glanced over her shoulder and stuck her arse out much further than was necessary when she leant across a table to wipe it down. It was the first time in my life I'd ever looked at another woman and thought – *little slut* – with approval. I gaped shamelessly at her tits and replayed in my mind the moment when she told me, 'I wanted to feel that mouth on me for real, God, I wanted it so, so bad.'

Little slut.

My mind went over all possible options, all possible escape

routes. There was no point trying to make a move until the end of service at ten o'clock. I had to wait. Even then we'd need to be very careful, although by that stage of the evening the front-of-house manager Elias was often drunk enough that he'd forget all about his staff, intent as he always was on telling a captive audience his life story, with flourishes, sighs and the occasional tear.

At ten past ten I saw her disappearing into the passage that led to the toilets. I abandoned my half-cleared table and followed her.

She must have paused there because I was suddenly right on top of her. Grabbing her hand, I said, 'Quick.'

She let me pull her into the ladies'. I locked the door behind us.

The lavatories of this restaurant were meant to be a talking point. Both were small rooms housing a single toilet each, and both were decorated in an absurd rococo style with damson-red walls, erotic prints – homoerotic male chests in the ladies', gagged and bound women in the gents' – and swag velvet curtains around a floor-length mirror. These lavatories were staged to be scenes of illicit encounters. Elias liked to tell people how often he found the seats smeared with cocaine.

There was something in me that resented this set-up. It almost made me feel as if having a screw in this environment was a conventional thing to do.

Then I remembered that it wasn't meant for us. It wasn't our stage. We weren't customers. We were service hussies.

She was waiting, watching. I moved in and our mouths met. There was her smell, not a fragrance as such, not quite female and not quite male. It was the smell of her body, slightly salty and sweet and totally compelling. We kissed quietly and her tongue darted into my mouth, neat and precise. Just how I thought it would be.

There were fingers trailing down the side of my face, down my neck, over my shoulder. I concentrated on keeping my lips soft, kissing her with all the skill and sensitivity I could muster. Somehow I felt that for another woman I had to do this as well as I possibly could. There was nowhere to hide, unlike with a man, when raw passion and enthusiasm can always cover up clumsiness. With Aia I had to get it right, and maybe I did, because she rewarded me with a cute little sound that came from the back of her throat into mine.

She started to undo my shirt buttons and I did the same to her, spreading her shirt front open and covering her tits with my hands. They were surprisingly large on her small frame, weighing down the stretchy cups of her T-shirt bra. With a smile I left her face and moved downwards so that she could feel my mouth on her for real.

She was already undoing her bra for me. I helped her take it off, along with her shirt, and then I applied myself to the job of pleasuring her tits. I began by drawing a big circle with my tongue, running wide round one nipple but not touching it. I went round again, and again, my circles getting gradually smaller but still keeping clear of the centre. She leant against the wall and pushed her ribcage forward. I used the very tip of my tongue to make a final few circles and then I landed on her nipple, a solid nubbin of flesh that seemed, from her reaction, to be extraordinarily sensitive, causing her to bite her lips together to stifle her moans.

I sucked her quite hard, but not too hard, now and then breaking away to fret her with my tongue tip. I moved to her other breast. She plunged her fingers into my hair and cradled the back of my skull. I sank to my knees and found I was at the perfect height to come at her tits from underneath and graze them with my teeth and feel their velvety warm weight on my face. And I was at the perfect height to tuck my hand between her legs, where the heat and damp seeped through her black trousers.

I recognised that dampness. It was something I had felt on myself many times. There was so much that was familiar in this foreign situation.

Back arched, Aia was moving against the wall as if something had already entered her. She placed her hand on top of mine, demonstrating the stroke and the pressure she liked. I broke away from her tit and looked up, seeing her ribs and the underside of her breasts and the naked hollow of her underarm.

'Hey, Aia,' I said, hearing the strain in my voice as I rubbed as hard as I could.

'Mm?'

'I haven't asked you my other question yet.'

'What's the question?' she replied, eyes closed, breathing heavily.

'Will you show me what you did?'

'What did I do? When?'

'When you were thinking of me.'

Her eyes opened momentarily, then closed again.

'Don't stop,' she said.

Then her face broke into a grin.

I kept up the pressure on her crotch but soon I started to get impatient. It was beginning to look as though Aia was going for broke on my hand, and I hadn't even got her fly undone yet. So I unzipped her and, just as I was beginning to pull down her trousers, she grabbed my wrists.

'That's quite enough,' she said. 'Into the corner with you.'

There was nothing in me that wanted to resist so I let her push me into the corner of the cubicle and I stayed there, the mirror cold on the back of my shoulders, as she returned to the far corner, just out of reach.

Her eyes darted down to my tits, spilling out of my bra cups that she'd pushed aside like curtains not long ago. Pursing her lips she smiled.

'You are going to love this,' she said.

The supreme certainty of this announcement made me catch my breath and squeeze my legs together. She had the naughtiest imaginable smile, and threw me a burlesque wink as she inched her trousers down with a knowing slowness, tits and hips swaying. I was so turned on, my snatch was roaring, but I was transfixed by what I was seeing and didn't think to touch myself.

She sat on the toilet seat to take her trousers right off, leaving her black suede ankle boots on. Sitting very upright she looked at me with her brow slightly lowered. Hands resting on her knees, she opened her legs wide. The flimsiest strip of black nylon lace lay over her vulva.

Oh, but she looked perfect, with a face full of determination and a soft sheen on her thighs, half her hair escaping from her ponytail. Her eyes darted between me and the mirror next to me. Her hands began to move, sweeping up her legs, one heading for her breast, the other for her pussy, slipping inside her knickers. I could see on her face the little jolt of pleasure when she touched her clit: a blink and a smile and an indrawn breath. I could picture how it must have felt. I could relate to that smile and the smooth action of her hands, one stroking her slit, one pinching and pulling her nut-brown nipple.

And it struck me that this was exactly how Aia wanted it. She liked being watched, being chased by eyes. She wanted me to love her from a distance. Her ego was massive and magnificent. There was a slight shaking in her shoulders and legs as she leant back further, opening her body up more. I was getting tantalising glimpses of her labia, appearing and disappearing as her hand moved, and I fought the urge to launch myself over there and rip those annoying knickers off her.

The door handle rattled as someone tried to get in. Aia jumped, frowned, shook her head in a dismissive way and resumed her wank. The handle rattled again and someone knocked on the door.

Aia's eyes met mine. I held my breath and listened.

It might have been a customer, but the brisk and businesslike way those knuckles were rapping the wood suggested it could well have been Elias looking for his absent waitresses.

For a moment I wondered if the game was up. Should we get our clothes back on quickly and try to pretend we'd been in there for some legitimate reason? Perhaps one of us could fake up a few tears, as if we'd been in the middle of some sudden emotional crisis? But if he didn't buy it we'd be instantly sacked, and he'd probably even keep our tips, knowing Elias.

Aia was nearly naked. Her clothes were all over the cubicle. Her hair was a mess. It would take ages for her to get ready. I wasn't too bad – I still had my trousers on – but what about Aia?

I heard a man clear his throat on the other side of the door, inches away from me.

'Girls?'

It was Elias.

My hands were hurting. I realised that my fists were clenched and my fingernails were digging into my palms to force myself to stay quiet.

Elias coughed again awkwardly.

'Girls, you in there?' he said again, from slightly further away.

He was wavering in the corridor, obviously unsure whether the toilet was occupied by customers. Aia and I looked at each other and suddenly it was very hard not to burst out laughing.

'Ah,' said Elias. 'Hm.'

Aia gave me another wink then bent her neck, bringing her face down to her breast which she pushed upwards with her hand, the other hand moving again in her knickers. Her long, purplish tongue came out, as obscene as anything I'd ever seen in my life. She held my gaze as she licked herself, her tongue at full stretch, nudging at the very tip of her nipple, flicking from side to side to build sensation.

I couldn't hold back any longer. I dropped to my knees in front of her. I tore her knickers off and threw them aside. Wedging my hand down inside my trousers I leant in and took my first long, slow lick of her pussy.

What I found there was Aia in concentrated form, slippery and beyond delicious. What amazed me was how alive, how responsive she was down there, her clit growing and growing under my mouth, her juices flowing down my chin. It was shocking to have such close contact with something so new, another woman's clit, something I'd only ever seen in porn. The sheer sensory overload drove me wild. I had a finger between my own pussy lips, dabbing away madly as I licked and sucked and snogged her pussy with enthusiasm bordering on delirium and no finesse whatsoever. I don't think she minded my clumsiness too much. It was the way she clasped my head with both hands and gripped my hair and rocked her snatch into my face that made me relax about it completely, so that I was only vaguely aware of the strange gasps and grunts I was making. I was only vaguely aware of the lack of oxygen and the crazy heat in my cheeks that were clamped between her wet inner thighs. I was in heaven itself. Whether Elias was still out there, listening through the door, I didn't even consider. Even if he had crossed my mind I wouldn't have cared a jot for my job, my dignity or my tips. Playing this soft, soft morsel with my tongue I felt as if there was something happening in this ludicrously decorated room that was very good, very secret, and really, really pervy.

I found her hole and slid two fingers up inside, as easy as anything. My God, it was hot up there, and there was a definite, gradual tightening, ever so slight, ever so gentle, the kind of feeling I could really relate to, shrinking round my fingers as I drew them out and dipped them in. Her thighs relaxed and dropped a little, allowing me to look up the length of her. Her mouth was open and her lids so heavy I could barely make eye contact. I picked up the pace, thrusting a little harder, and her legs opened up more. She was pushing her weight downwards onto my hand. Screwing her more and more vigorously I had the idea that I should lighten up on her clit a little, so I pulled my head back and just laid my tongue lightly on her, allowing only the smallest movement, imagining that it was just the right counterpoint to give her.

And then it happened, right in my face, with an abrupt escalation of noise and thrust, with a rattling of ceramic as she arched her back and pushed against the cistern with such force I thought she was going to knock the lid off. And then, as she came back down and her limbs relaxed, she did knock the lid off. It crashed onto the floor and broke into several large pieces and a shower of china splinters.

'Oh dear,' I said. 'That was a bit loud.'

Biting her lip Aia looked around herself.

I fingered my slit, feeling slightly mournful because I realised it was time to get dressed and start thinking up excuses. I had no doubt whatsoever that Elias would be at the door within seconds.

Aia jumped to her feet, full of energy again.

'OK,' she said. 'OK, OK. Action stations.'

And instead of starting to get her clothes on she grabbed my trousers and pulled them to my ankles along with my soaking wet knickers.

The door handle started to rattle.

'Aia,' I whispered.

'OK, OK.'

Standing up she whipped me round, pushed me down so I was sitting on the toilet seat, got carefully to her knees, swept some shards to one side, and pushed my legs open. Elias's knuckles were rapping the door as she parted my lips with two fingers of one hand and plunged two fingers of the other up inside me, making me gasp and grip the edges of the toilet seat. I was half-panicking and it felt amazing, so urgent, so inappropriate, as she stroked my clit with the edge of her thumb and thrust into my pussy at the same time.

'Hey, what's going on in there?' said Elias, sounding angry. 'I'd say that's enough of the good times, wouldn't you? We've got to clear up before someone gets hurt.'

I looked up and in the mirror I could see us both, surrounded by lank velvet curtains, plaster scrolls painted dull gold and glinting ceramic fragments. Naughty Aia had placed herself slightly to one side of me which allowed me to see everything, the gleam on her fingers, the shuddering of my legs, the glow of my reddened hole. Her tits leant over me. The certainty of coming was flitting round peripherally, just within reach, then just beyond.

'Nearly,' I groaned.

'You in there, girls?' said Elias, his voice coming from right up against the door. 'Girls. I'm warning you. Those good times are going to cost you. I mean it.'

Her hands were taking such good care of my snatch. To feel and see it so graphically was almost too much. She was panting and breathing heavily, willing me on. I was so, so close and she leant over and lapped at my nipple with her filthy purple tongue.

I must have shut my eyes at that point because all I was aware of was this chain reaction bursting all down me. I must

171

have been loud. I don't remember. All I recall is opening my eyes to the sound of a thudding fist on the door.

'I got customers here who need to *piss*,' shouted Elias.

After that it went quiet in the corridor while Aia and I tidied ourselves up, sorted our clothes and got dressed. We didn't rush. Elias didn't bother us any more. He must have retreated back into the restaurant. He'd be waiting for us at the bar, fiddling angrily with the stem of his wineglass, calculating whether he should fire us immediately or wait until the end of the night when we'd finished the mopping and emptied the bins.

Before we unlocked the door we took a last look at each other's flushed faces.

The good times were going to cost us. The wink she threw me told me Aia didn't care.

Ticking Over
by Carmel Lockyer

I know you, I thought, looking at my passenger in the rearview mirror. *I've seen you somewhere before.*

She glanced up and caught my eye and I knew that if I'd been a male driver, she'd have glared at me, telling me to back off. Women travelling alone are really nervous about taxi drivers these days, which is one reason I get so much work. Because I'm a woman, she just gave me a quick social smile and looked down at her briefcase again.

I still knew that I knew her, from somewhere. A junior government minister? No, too well groomed. A TV weathergirl? No ... too old, but in a good way, in a crinkles-around-her-eyes, knowing-what-she-wants-and-how-to-get-it kind of way. Nope, it nagged and it niggled but I couldn't work out how I recognised her.

I pulled out into traffic, whistling tunelessly through my teeth in accepted London cab driver style. It was all an act, like her busy career woman pretence. I was actually knackered, completely cream-crackered, having spent half the night logged into Gong-Bangers, even eating my takeaway curry with the laptop balanced on my knees so as not to miss a second of the various shows going on. There was one woman with blue-black hair that snaked over her shoulders, down to her breasts, hiding her nipples, but in no way concealing the astonishing jet-black Brazilian that punctuated her mons. She swayed to a music I couldn't hear and turned, revealing beautiful dimpled buttocks with her inky hair swinging and bouncing over her spine, before returning to face the camera and leaning forward, pale nipples sliding into view as she chatted online. In a corner of my screen the messages popped up. Her "name" was Sirene and watchers called Mojo, Adelaide and Ginny begged her to spread her legs, suck her fingers, wiggle her arse ... But I'm too shy to talk to women like Sirene, even via a webcam and chatroom.

The thing is, I just knew I recognised this passenger from somewhere, even in my sleep-deprived state. It was really starting to annoy me, so I kept up the meaningless chit-chat that taxi drivers are supposed to provide, as I flicked my eyes over her, using the rearview mirror to refresh my memory.

She bent her head over her documents, tucking her dark hair behind her ear with a ringless left hand and I remembered where I'd seen her. Or at least where I imagined I had, because I must have made a mistake. Surely I had ...

A few weeks ago there had been a woman on Gong-Bangers – a little older than the average, a little less femme. She'd worn an oyster-coloured satin nightshirt, formal and severe in styling, but not thick enough to hide the wide, dark nipples that pressed against the fabric, nor the darker patch between her legs, barely glimpsed as the shirt moved in response to her shaking body. For she was nervous, despite her defiantly raised chin and the arms folded beneath her breasts. The tiny vibrations of her fear made the sheer cloth shimmy over her hips and thighs. I found myself leaning closer to the screen, willing her to speak.

Instead she leant over too, and pressed a button out of sight of her webcam. Slow, smoky music came tinnily through my speakers. Billie Holiday crooning something about violets and furs.

From her nervousness, and the unflirtatious style of her clothing, I wouldn't have expected her to be much of a mover – but she was. Either she was a natural exhibitionist or a trained dancer, and I'd have put my money on her being both. She was no longer self-conscious, in fact it was almost as if she'd forgotten the camera was there and a couple of times she moved out of its range, causing me to hiss with disappointment. I could imagine women all over the world, howling at their computer screens as she slipped from view.

She unbuttoned the nightshirt slowly, swaying and turning, singing along to the music with her eyes closed, twin fans of chocolate-brown lashes resting on peachy skin. When her eyes opened again, her pupils were large and dark and I moaned, willing her to slide the shirt from her shoulders to reveal the dark discs of her nipples, her navel, the triangle at her thighs. Instead she turned her back to the camera, tucking her hair behind her ear with the gesture I'd recognised when I saw it again, and then held her arms wide, shaking her hidden backside in my face like a threat … or a promise.

She snapped the nightshirt out around her like a flag, the whip-crack echoing through the speakers. My hands were locked around the arms of my computer chair, willing, insisting, begging her to take it off. Slowly, glancing over one shoulder and then the other, she eased the garment down her arms so her beautiful spine was displayed. Then she turned, shyness gone, to show the viewers her breasts. The merciless light – where was she? A kitchen, an operating theatre? – deprived her skin of shadows. Even so, she was glorious, right from the mother-of-pearl cleft between her breasts to her deeply indented navel.

'More,' I whispered to the screen, sure I could hear the rest of her audience whispering with me.

The creamy fabric was caught together by a single button below her navel, barely hiding the dark patch further down. The cloth gathered in folds and creases under her breasts and pulled into taut bands over her well-muscled upper arms. I had never in my life wished so much to be able to reach into the computer and twitch and tug the garment away.

And here she was again, in front of me, or rather, behind me, as untouchably framed in my rearview mirror as she'd been in the computer screen. If only I could remember the name she'd used on Gong-Bangers! But even if I did, what could I say to her? I was absolutely no good at talking to women – that's why I paid the hefty membership for exclusive online access to natural, normal women who simply enjoyed showing their bodies to other women.

My fare tutted at something on her laptop, and I realised I'd been driving on autopilot. I jumped back into the real world – checking the meter and both wing mirrors before glancing into the rearview again. I was sure it was her. What had she been calling herself?

Then again, I didn't have to remember her screen name – there were other ways I could indicate my knowledge to her.

'Nice laptop,' I said, nodding towards it.

'Thank you.' She didn't look up.

'I'm more of a flat-screen fan myself,' I said. 'Webcam, all that stuff, you know?'

She shrugged, casting me a glance in the rearview mirror, her dark eyes as cold as iced coffee. And the chilly glance gave me her name, as clearly as if she'd said it aloud – Mocha!

I grinned to myself as we pulled up to a red light. Mocha. And after the brief teasing moment when she'd stood with her oyster nightshirt and waited for her audience to beg and plead, she'd simply shrugged, just as she had a moment ago in the cab, and the cloth fell away to leave her naked.

Her mouth and nipples were like overripe plums, dark and sweet, and her mound was generously covered in jet-black curls, each neat and glossy as if a top hairstylist had just set them in place.

'More, more,' bayed the watchers, their messages of pleasure and suggestions of further intimacies scrolling across the bottom of the screen.

And then, as sometimes happened, my screen went black. I cursed, tapping my fingers in the mouse until the "Activate Webcam" message appeared. It was a random check to ensure that the person watching the show was the same person who'd paid the massive membership fee. I snapped on the webcam and read out the sentence that appeared on my screen. The unknown security person, or robot maybe, obviously accepted that I was the same stocky, square-jawed, blue-eyed butch who'd appeared in the video clip Gong-Bangers had captured during my membership interview. He, she, or it flicked me back to the action.

Mocha was gone. I stared in horror at the screen, where a

kittenish Asian girl was now playing with an orange dildo. How far had Mocha gone while I was being security checked? Was she coming back? Had she given a time or date for her next show?

Since then I'd been watching Gong-Bangers whenever I could, eating in front of the screen, dozing off in my computer chair, but Mocha had never reappeared.

Until now. Until she'd slipped into my cab, all business, acting like an ice-princess with attitude, but I knew better – there was no ice in those veins: it was pure caffeine, adrenaline and "look at me" exhibitionism that filled her body. Mocha – the kind of dream that kept a woman awake all night.

Too soon we were there. Her destination was one of those silvery boxes designed by an architect to look like an ice cube, and for a moment I imagined the sheer hot sexuality of Mocha, hidden beneath her executive clothing, melting the building as she walked into it, so that her clothes were made wet and clinging, embracing her body the way I wanted to.

Her company had an account, so I didn't even get to touch her hand as she gave me a tip, and as I pulled back into the traffic, I felt sick. Twice I'd let Mocha slip away from me, and now I might never see her again, virtually or in the flesh. Was I a woman or a mouse?

I'd gone less than half a mile when it was too much for me. I pulled off the road and sat for a few minutes with my eyes closed, remembering the hot Mocha who'd stripped for strangers on a webcam and the iced Mocha who'd sat in my cab like a robot. Why would a woman like Mocha get her kit off online? She could have snapped her fingers and had a dozen lovers falling at her feet: male, female, whatever she wanted. Was it possible that she found it as difficult as me to talk to other women?

I tilted the rearview mirror to look at myself. OK, I wasn't a great looker, but I was in shape, I had good teeth and my hair was short and neat ... I was OK. And I might never again meet a woman like Mocha in the flesh, a dream made real, and it was up to me to decide if I had the guts to try and make the dream come true. Or just make the dream come.

The play on words made me grin at my reflection. I thought about calling Dispatch and saying I had an engine problem and would be taking the rest of the day off, but then they'd just try and get me to take another car out, so I simply ignored the squawking radio calls, shoved the cab into gear and headed for New Covent Garden Market where I bought all the flowers I could afford, a bottle of champagne and two glasses.

I drove back to the ice cube like a madwoman and sat outside, one eye on the entrance, the other concentrating on ripping the flowerheads off their stems and chucking them into the back of the cab where they hit the seat or floor at random. The scent of freesias and carnations, rose petals and lilies filled the enclosed space and I imagined Mocha's milky limbs crushing their cool softness into liquid pleasure. I pictured myself tearing sunshiny marigolds to pieces and sprinkling their vibrant petals into her black pubes before licking them out again with the tip of my tongue.

The idea that I was only going to get one shot at success made my heart knock in my chest like some small creature trapped in a box. I was pinning everything on her not having booked a cab for the return journey because there was nothing logged on the system as a forward booking for her company, but she could be staying in there all day, or perhaps she liked to walk home after a meeting – if I'd got it wrong, I'd wasted a fortune on flowers and fizz and I'd never see Mocha again.

But no, after an hour or so, there she was, striding out of the building, tucking her hair behind her ears, looking up and down the street. *Head north*, I thought, *north is where I want you to go ...*

And she did. I pulled back into the traffic, zooming past her and skidding to a stop outside a coffee shop I'd already earmarked. I half ran inside and yelled out my order like a madwoman, then slapped a tenner on the counter, grabbed my two takeaway mochas and ran, not waiting for my change. Back in the cab I slotted the hot drinks into the cup holders that I used during night shifts and waited for Mocha to walk past me.

I pulled back into the traffic, cruising slowly until I was

level with her, then I hit the window button and my horn simultaneously so that she looked over.

'Excuse me,' I said. 'I just wondered if you fancied ...' Her face was stony and I faltered. '... fancied a coffee? I mean a mocha. I mean ...'

She stopped walking. I felt my heart drumming again.

'Mocha?' she said.

'Oh yes, it's my favourite.' I was babbling and I knew it, but at least she'd spoken. 'You can't find a better drink – strong and sweet and very sexy.'

'Sexy?' Her eyes widened and she almost smiled. I grinned back.

'Oh yes, a mocha's the sexiest thing on Earth, except perhaps ...'

'Perhaps?' Now she was definitely smiling.

Instead of answering I leant back and flicked open the door of the cab. I didn't even glance behind me, I just watched the look on her face as flowers fell out into the street and the wave of scent hit her. Those big dark eyes, never bigger, never darker, that smile, never softer or more mysterious – I'd seen it once onscreen but now it was aimed at me.

'Please,' I said. 'I would like to cover you with flowers and toast you in champagne, but to start with, we could drive to Battersea Park and drink these mochas before moving into the back of the cab so I can make love to you until the tyres melt with lust.'

Tyres melt with lust? What kind of corny line was that? But Mocha didn't seem to mind; instead she tucked her hair behind her ear and smiled down at the ground before tapping her fingertips on the cab door. 'How did you know I didn't suffer from hay fever?'

My mouth dropped open. I'd never thought she might be allergic to flowers. She laughed out loud before opening the door and slipping into the passenger seat.

I was glad that it was nearly evening, and dusk was close. All around me, as I drove to Battersea, cars were putting on their headlights. As long as I proceeded slowly, I might have the cover of darkness to seduce her.

What was her name? Could I call her Mocha? Suddenly I was embarrassed and unsure and found my eyes locking on the road ahead, too shy to glance over at her, but in my peripheral vision I saw her hand reach out for the cup of mocha and sip it as we moved sedately through the rush-hour traffic. When she replaced the cup in the holder she flicked my ID which was pinned to the dashboard. 'Rosa?'

I nodded, eyes on the road.

'Pretty name,' she said.

'Not as pretty as Mocha,' I replied, and then blushed. I didn't dare look over until she laughed out loud.

'I've been caught, haven't I?' Her laughter was as rich and dark as her name.

I nodded. 'I only saw you once, but that was enough – I could never forget you.'

'I only did it once.' She tucked her hair behind her ear again and sighed. I dared to glance over.

'Why do it at all then?'

'Oh, it was a mad, exciting adventure, but I couldn't repeat it. I didn't have the nerve.'

And then I told her everything. How I'd been seduced from the first moment I saw her but how the security scan had taken me away from her performance at the last and worst possible moment. As I talked and drove, I watched her profile, seeing the colour rise in her cheeks as I described her body to her, telling her how lush and elegant she was, how enticing and svelte. I pretended I was talking to the screen on which I'd seen her, rather than to Mocha herself, and the words poured out until we arrived at the park and I pulled the cab in under the willow trees.

I got out and opened the back door, releasing that intense fragrance again. Mocha slipped from the car and stood beside me, her shoulder touching mine and I took her fingers and tugged her gently into the back seat.

It would be a lie to say everything went smoothly. To begin with I was worried about ruining Mocha's suit, but she didn't give a damn, and as she wriggled the skirt up her thighs, I definitely heard a seam rip but she simply grinned like a naughty girl. She was wearing neutral-coloured hold-ups with lacy tops and I nearly lost control of myself when I saw them appearing as the skirt hem was tugged up. I followed her into the cab, slammed the door behind me, and knelt on the floor as her white cotton knickers, stretched tight across the sable pubes, came into sight. I didn't even bother to pull them out of the way, I just tongued her through the fabric until her lips swelled and her clit pressed against the wet cloth and I couldn't tell if the juice came from my mouth or from her, everything was so slick and shiny and tasting of flowers and sex.

When she came she shuddered, her thighs bracing against the seat, her arms outstretched along the back like a crucified Venus. When she came again she arched her back so my hands slid right under her pearly arse and helped to lift her body into my face. When she came the third time she made a sound like a violin string breaking, like a body stretched beyond pain and pleasure, like an angel crying.

The windows of the cab were steamed up like the Ironmonger Row Turkish bath on ladies' night. Under my knees and under her thighs lay a smear of petals like heaven's carpet. Over our heads the willows moving as gently as Mocha's breathing as she relaxed back into the seat, her head drooping, dark wings of hair framing her pink cheeks and soft, inky eyes. I put my arm around her, pulling her forwards onto my fingers and, as I entered her swollen wetness, she sighed and I almost thought I saw her breath in the cab like the steam rising from hot coffee. I opened her as easily as blinking, and she moved herself around with short curling motions like a spoon in a cup until she came again, her head back, her neck strained as she stared sightless into her own ecstasy.

And then, in the silence that followed, I heard a tiny sound. My meter had clicked over. I turned my head and looked over my shoulder. In all the fear and excitement I'd forgotten to turn it off, and it had just hit a figure it had never reached before. I pulled Mocha's head down to mine and kissed her deeply, sliding my tongue around her teeth and into her cheeks to explore every inch of her I could reach. According to the meter she'd cost me £400 in lost fares. Her hands gripped my shoulders and slid down my arms as she pulled back from the kiss to nibble my neck.

It had been worth every penny.

Carny Girl
by Lynn Lake

She worked the bumper car ride, flipping the switch that electrified the ride, untangling cars, telling off over-aggressive teenagers, cleaning up after overexcited kids. She was black – dark black – with straight slick hair, a lean, sinewy body, and a hard, pretty face. She wore skintight faded jeans and a green tank-top, studs in her nose and rings in her nipples, which poked almost right through the thin material of her top.

I first saw her on the Friday afternoon when the travelling carnival opened up for the long weekend. And by Friday night, I was totally infatuated.

I'd never seen anyone like her, thanks to my small-town Indiana upbringing; the way she looked, the way she moved, the way she told off the boys, and men, who rode the ride too hard, or got too fresh with the operator. As I watched her go about her work with utter confidence and contempt, black velvet skin gleaming under the hot sun, taut muscles tightening and rippling, an ache – a soul-searing need – to be loved by this hardboiled woman throbbed inside me.

'Fuck you always hangin' around for?' she asked me Saturday morning. 'Ride or glide, blondie.'

I flushed beet-red, twisting one of my pigtails around in my fingers and staring down at the cracked, littered ground. I was just a plump little girly-girl from the country, and she was … something else entirely; I had no idea how to approach her, how to converse with her. 'Uh, I guess I'll, um … ride?' I gulped.

'Then set your ass down,' she stated, unsmiling.

I stumbled onto the metal platform, kids screaming and rushing past me, racing for the best cars.

Her nametag read "Mya", and when every last car was taken, kids giggling and yelling with anticipation, she did a quick walk-around. 'Seatbelt, blondie!' she snapped at me.

I'd forgotten to lock myself in, too busy gazing at Mya's taut, twitching bum, her hard little shuddering breasts and shining face. She reached down and yanked my strap over my shoulder, buckled it down at my waist. Then her hand hummed up and down the frayed nylon to make sure it was secure, her long dark fingers brushing against one of my stiffened nipples, shooting sparks all through me.

She leant in close, and the spicy scent of her body filled my senses, her teeth blazing white in a grin. 'You're good an' tight now, blondie. If you wasn't already.'

I dazedly watched her walk off, my body and being tingling with longing.

She flipped the switch and my car jumped. Kids sailed all around, occasionally banging into me, or cursing me for just sitting there. But I hardly noticed, looking over at Mya standing tall and lean and sexy on the edge of the platform, looking back at me.

Sunday afternoon, when she went on her break, I followed her. Past the trailers and trucks and across the field to a dilapidated barn that stood on the far edge of the fairground, next to a stand of trees. Her shoulders and hips moved with an animal ease and litheness, oiled in sensuality. She didn't look back, but I knew she knew I was trailing after her. She slipped in behind the barn, and I heard voices.

I crept along the side of the weathered building, holding my breath, peeked around the corner. And my heart sank, my eyes welling with hot, bitter tears. Mya was down on her knees on the yellowed grass, in front of a big brassy redhead. Her dark hands gripped the woman's pale thighs, her neon-pink tongue lapping at the woman's ginger pussy.

I bit my lip, my fingernails gouging into the wood. The redhead's skirt and panties were tangled around her ankles, her legs spread, with Mya in between, licking and licking and licking at the woman's pussy. Her head bobbed rapidly and rhythmically up and down, her long tongue stroking the woman from bottom to top, bumhole to clit.

Blood spurted out of my lower lip and wetted my teeth, splinters gathering at my whitened fingertips. As the redhead tore her blouse and bra open and grabbed up her milky tits. She anxiously squeezed them, pinched the thick pink nipples, rolling her head back and forth against the barn – Mya's unceasing cunt-lapping filling her with the heated joy to match my heated hate.

I wanted to scream, to rush forward and pummel that bitch who was getting so much – everything – from my three-day-old girlfriend, the love of my young life. But I did nothing, but watch, fat tears rolling down my chubby cheeks, as Mya openly and obscenely ate out that woman right in front of me.

She planted her face in the redhead's glistening pussy and sucked on the woman's clit. The woman gasped, moaned, her huge tits jumping in her clutching hands. Mya's cheeks hollowed, lips working, tongue tripping the woman's trigger, and setting her off.

'Oh, God, yes!' she cried, shivering, quivering, coming in my Mya's mouth.

I could barely stand, my legs were so weak, my rage and lust impotent forces, as usual.

But Mya stood up, easily. Wiping her mouth off, she demanded, '50 bucks, bitch.'

The redhead slapped her, indignant at being called a bitch. Mya grinned, and slapped her back, bouncing the woman's head off the barn. I gasped, glaring at the heated scene.

The woman brushed her hair back from her reddened face and buttoned up her blouse, pulled up her skirt. Then she fumbled around in her purse and handed $50 over to Mya. 'Tonight?' she asked, looking up shyly.

Mya laughed, nodded, sticking the money in her jeans.

The redhead ran my way, and I ducked back behind the corner of the barn, hugging the boards, even more shaken. Because in that instant, I'd actually gotten a good look at the woman's face – it was Mrs Hufnagel, wife of the chief of

185

police. She had three kids, was in our church choir. She ran past me in her low heels and back to the Midway, not even noticing me in her haste.

'You got 50 bucks too, blondie?' I jumped. It was Mya, right next to me.

'Uh, um …' I dug a hand into a pocket of my jean shorts, knowing full well I didn't have that much money. But I was talking to Mya, at last, in private.

'Didn't think so,' she sneered. 'Then you're givin', girl, not gettin'.'

She grabbed my arm and pulled me around the side of the barn, shoved me up against the wood almost exactly where Mrs Hufnagel had taken her licking. Then she pinned my arms up above my head with her strong hands and pushed her face in close to mine. Her large brown eyes burned into my unblinking baby-blues, her hot breath flooding my open mouth.

The heat from her body so close set me to shimmering with desire, the hard pointed tips of her breasts touching the buzzing tips of my breasts. She slid her pink tongue out and washed her thick lips with it, nostrils flaring, eyes narrowing. 'You're a real Barbie girl, huh, blondie? Still in her original packaging.' She laughed in my face.

I was dizzy, almost delirious. This *would* be my first time with a real woman … 'Start lickin', girl!' Mya hissed. 'I only got ten minutes left.'

She shoved me down to my knees and skinned her jeans down, stuck her pussy right into my face. Stunned, I grabbed onto her bare hips and tentatively stuck my tongue into her tangle of fur, the heady aroma of her sex making my head spin and resolve weaken. She gripped my pigtails and jerked my head forward, burying my face in her jungle pussy.

I couldn't believe she was as wet as I was. I squirmed my tongue against her moistened pussy lips, and she jumped. My pink-painted fingernails bit into her smooth noir skin, as I boldly plunged my tongue right inside her cunt.

I had no experience; I didn't know what I was doing. But it seemed to be working, because as I thrashed my tongue around in her hot wet tunnel, warm, tangy liquid suddenly flooded my mouth. I peered upward, into Mya's eyes.

'Dirty little corn-fed slut,' she said, grinning down at me.

Mya pulled her tank-top off and my hands up, plastering them onto her bare breasts, her juices flowing out from between her trembling legs and drenching my beaming face. I grasped her firm breasts and rolled her jutting, ringed nipples between my fingers, gulping some of her juice now, straight from her pussy.

It was exhilarating, intoxicating. I couldn't get enough, groping Mya's tits and bathing in her come, drinking it in. As she urged me on with an equal stream of profanity.

Until, finally, she yelled, 'Fuck!' She desperately clenched her buttocks and another gush of liquid glided into my open mouth. Then I pulled one of my hands off her tits and stuck three fingers into her slit, and pumped.

'Yeah, blondie!' she wailed. 'Fuck me!'

I clutched at her breasts and slammed my fingers back and forth in her cunt, the wanton taste of the woman empowering me with heedless lust. I was on fire, pistoning her pussy, her hot pink wetness sucking on my fingers.

'Fuck! Jesus!' she cried, bending, breaking on my flying digits.

She gushed all over again, the pure product of *my* efforts; I couldn't believe one girl could come so much. And I licked, urgently swallowed, churning her cunt. Until she fully sagged over on top of me, gasping for breath.

I never went back to the travelling carnival. That was kids' stuff now.

I never saw Mya again, either. That kind of adult stuff I could now get all on my own.

Dress Rehearsal
by Jean-Philippe Aubourg

'No, no! More passion! Make me feel your raw animal lust!'
Jen broke away from Rachel, their lips parting with a soft
smack. The two naked women turned to look at Claude.

'I need to believe. I need to be convinced. I need to know
that right now nothing matters more to either of you than
satisfying your carnal desires with this beautiful woman.'

'You could have hired real lesbians,' said Rachel. She and
Jen giggled, but Claude was not amused.

'I hired actresses, or at least I thought I had – actresses who
could convince an audience of the inner truth of a play.'

'It takes time, Claude, especially with sex scenes. You have
to feel completely comfortable with the other person.' Jen
shifted round on the bed which she and Rachel were lying on.
Their legs had been wrapped around each other, thigh to hip,
and their arms around one another's shoulders. Now they
turned to face their director.

'We've been rehearsing for a week and we open in another
two. We don't have time,' he said abruptly. That was true.
Conceived, written and cast in a fortnight, this play was a
sprint, not a marathon. The collapse of a production company
behind another play had left a small North London theatre with
a three-week hole in its calendar. They had approached Claude,
a young writer-director who liked to push boundaries, and he
could not resist the challenge.

His work always had impact, but this time he was
determined to be noticed. Freed from the constraint of having
to find a theatre and convince it to stage his new play, he

189

allowed his imagination to run wild. What his imagination came up with was a love story with a twist. He wanted to explore the concept of attraction and sexual desire, and he wanted to do this through the story of two previously heterosexual women who decided to defy convention and try lesbianism.

Casting was a problem. Only actresses who had experience of stage nudity were asked to audition. There were plenty of those, but many recoiled at what Claude was asking them to do. Some did not even respond to their agents' enquiry, some agents even refused to put the idea to their clients. Of those that came, many only made it up to the point when Claude asked them to strip. One even threw the script at him, shouting, 'This is disgusting!' before storming out. Of those who did take off their clothes, most were not up to the acting standard he required. He saw many models who aspired to be actresses and, gorgeous as they were, he was not making porn. Then he found Jen.

Jen had been out of work for three months. She was talented, but the parts had not been coming her way. When her agent sent her the script she was delighted, and said yes to the audition before reading it. After all, an audition was an audition. In between office temping and commuting she did not have time to study it, so only opened it as she boarded the Northern Line tube on her way to the theatre.

By the time she surfaced in Islington she was shaking. Could she really do this? Playing a lesbian was fine, kissing another girl, well, she would have been very naïve to think she could be a successful actress and not have to do that once or twice, and she had taken her clothes off for a role on more than one occasion. But the level of nudity in this play was off the scale! And not just nudity. The writer clearly wanted the audience to be in no doubt about the physical nature of the women's relationship. Two sex scenes, one which would probably take about ten minutes, when the character she was auditioning for was first seduced by the other woman, and another, even longer scene, when the affair came to a passionate but inevitable end.

190

Jen was always nervous at auditions, but this was something else. She trembled as she held the script, and could feel her voice shaking as she read through the lines with Claude. Like many directors, especially one taking the helm of his own play, he was somewhat aloof, treating his material with reverence. Jen was certain she had not got the job, so when he announced it was time for her to take her clothes off, she assumed it was just a formality. There was no way she was ever going to have to act this script in front of an audience, so let's just get it over with.

Putting down the script, she sat down to unzip her boots and pull them off. Standing again, she pulled her jumper over her head and dropped it onto the chair behind her. It was closely followed by her T-shirt. Opening her jeans, she pushed them down and stepped out of them, adding them to the pile of clothes. She felt goosebumps as the cold air of the unheated theatre surrounded her. Now she was standing in her bra, panties and pink ankle socks. Claude watched her, his expression giving nothing away. Was he still seriously assessing her for the part? Was she getting further away from it with every garment she removed? Was he getting hard at the sight of this attractive late-20s actress, with her short blonde hair, undressing in front of him?

Jen took a deep breath and unclipped her bra. Her nipples hardened as it came down her arms and over her wrists. The cold, she told herself. Now her breasts were bare. Not large, but not small either, Jen was proud of them, although right now she could not have been more self-conscious. But there was one more step she had to take. Putting her fingers and thumbs beneath the waistband of her panties, she pushed them down and stepped out of them. Straightening up, they hung loosely in her right hand. She felt her pubic hair bristle as it was completely exposed to the cold air and she blushed. Turning to show her full nudity to Claude, she lifted her right leg and started to pull on the toe of her sock, but his voice stopped her. 'That's fine, thank you. I just needed to know that you could do it. The part's yours.'

Two days later Jen was sitting fully dressed alongside

Claude. Half the script was already lodged in her brain, with the other half well on its way. All she needed now was a co-star.

Claude had suggested she sit in on the audition. After all, there had to be chemistry between the cast to make this two-hander work, and time was running out. They were only seeing one young actress this morning. Jen, who prided herself on her professionalism, was surprised to find herself worried that she would be hotter than her. When Rachel arrived it did nothing to lessen her concern.

Although her CV boasted a three-year drama course and an impressive list of stage credits, she still looked like a model. Her long brown hair was perfectly styled and her make-up exquisite. As she shook hands with Claude and Jen, both could see the blood-red varnish on her impeccably manicured fingernails. Claude offered to take her coat and bag, but she asked if she could take them to the dressing room herself. She had a couple of things to prepare for the reading, she said.

They waited in patient silence for her, Claude in a seat halfway down the theatre, Jen on stage to read with Rachel, until the sound of gentle approaching feet came from the wings. Then Rachel took the stage. Both Claude and Jen's eyes widened.

Rachel had changed from her street clothes, and was now wearing a simple blue silk robe. In her right hand she held the script. 'Shall I take it from the top of page 30?' she asked innocently, projecting her voice to the back of the auditorium.

'Yes. Take it away,' Claude said, his voice quivering a little. Excited at what Rachel might do next, thought Jen, or at the prospect of finding his other cast member?

Rachel had cleverly chosen the first nude scene to read through, showing she was prepared to tackle the controversial material head-on. As they worked through it, Jen found her admiration growing. She had learnt the lines, hardly ever needing to glance down at the script. She had chosen her costume well too. In the scene both girls would be wearing nothing but robes.

They reached the critical moment. Rachel's character was

the one who pushed Jen's over the edge, which she did by slipping off her robe and kissing her. As they reached that point, Rachel dropped the script then undid the belt of her robe. Pulling it back from her shoulders then shrugging them to send it to the floor, she revealed what Jen and Claude had both known from the second she took the stage. She was stark naked.

Rachel's body was spectacular. Her large breasts had the are-they-aren't-they look of a pair which could have been the work of a skilled surgeon or could be natural. Her waist was trim, her arms and thighs bronzed and toned. Her hands came up to Jen's face and her fingers were soft as she pulled her towards her. Their mouths locked, gently at first, then insistently, Rachel deepening the kiss, her tongue starting to flick against Jen's lips. Lost in the drama, Jen was about to open them in return, when Claude's voice broke the scene.

'Brilliant! Rachel, the gig's yours if you want it!' Rachel immediately broke off the kiss, releasing Jen's face, and turned to Claude in the stalls.

'Oh yes! I'd love it!' She clapped her hands, making her wonderful breasts wobble slightly. She seemed to have completely forgotten she was naked.

Now they were trying to re-create the passion of that first kiss. A week into rehearsal, they were both off the page, but Claude was adamant there was something missing. He sighed and looked at his watch. 'I have a meeting with the theatre director, to bring him up to speed. I'll tell him everything's going wonderfully and he's got the biggest hit since *Jerusalem* on his hands. Let's call it a day. Can I leave you to lock up?'

'Of course. We'll get dressed and pack up'.

Claude fished in his pocket and pulled out the theatre keys, lobbing them gently onto the stage, where two robes were piled. Picking up his jacket and bag, he turned and walked up the aisle to the theatre exit, calling a last goodbye over his shoulder.

Jen got off the bed and went to retrieve the key. She bent forward to pick it up, but froze at the sound of Rachel's voice.

'This shouldn't be that difficult. You've got a *gorgeous*

arse! And the rest of you isn't too shabby either!'

Jen straightened and turned to face her. Rachel was lying back on the bed now, her left leg out straight, her right lifted and bent at the knee, showing her dark pubes. She propped herself up on her elbows and looked straight at Jen. 'Now that Claude's gone, why don't we try the scene again? Maybe it's him that's putting us off?'

'Oh, er, maybe? Do you think it'll help?' Jen had been naked since she arrived for work that morning, but suddenly she was very self-conscious of her nudity.

'I think it will. And I think a little exercise first will help us nail it.' Jen was no stranger to acting exercises, but there was something about the way Rachel said it that suggested it might be a little out of the ordinary.

Rachel eased herself up and got to her feet. 'Sit down,' she told Jen. The blonde pulled up the wooden chair which was part of the bedroom set. The cheap fabric felt rough against her bare bottom. 'Now watch me.'

Jen nodded. She was looking straight at the brunette, as if seeing her body for the first time. Rachel started to run her hands up and down herself, across her thighs, over her flat stomach, cupping her breasts, turning as she cupped her bottom cheeks, squeezing them and parting them ever so slightly, before allowing them to spring back into place. Rachel turned back to face Jen, and now her hands were on her inner thighs. Her fingers were inches from her sex. Suddenly she flexed them, and her labia parted. Jen stared and then looked up at Rachel's face.

'Go on,' Rachel whispered. 'Look, if you want to. There's no need to keep eye contact. You have my permission to stare at any part of my body you want.'

Jen swallowed hard. She let her eyes travel back from Rachel's beautiful brown eyes, over her figure and down to her sex. Rachel had pulled it a little further apart, the pink flesh inside peeping at her. Was she acting, Jen wondered, or was she watching the real Rachel? Was she pretending to enjoy herself, or was she really pleasuring herself, right here on the stage of the theatre?

Rachel stepped back towards the bed, and lowered herself onto it, her feet still on the floor. She parted her thighs and pulled her vagina further apart. Jen felt her heart pounding and could hear her own breath quickening. Rachel put her head back and let out a groan as her fingers intruded inside the soft lips. She lowered her head and spoke to Jen once more. 'I'm going to masturbate, and you're going to watch me. Everyone does it; it's perfectly normal, but no one talks about it. Share the experience with me and we'll set this stage alight.'

Jen could not answer, but only watch as Rachel lay back and lifted her heels onto the woollen blanket which covered it. Her legs parted and Jen saw the fingers of her right hand start to rub her clit in small circles. At the same time she eased the first and second fingers of her left hand inside her, a little at first, then with more enthusiasm as her excitement heightened.

Through her parted legs Jen could see Rachel's hard nipples rising and falling higher and higher. Soon her fingers were burrowing deep inside, her other hand rubbing furiously, moving her clitoris in violent little circles. In less than a minute Rachel was moaning loudly and her body tensed and twitched violently. Eventually she was still.

Finally she looked up and eyed Jen from between her legs. 'Has that loosened a few of your acting muscles?' she asked, as she stroked her pubis with both hands. 'Shall we have another go at the scene?'

'In a moment. Something I have to do first.' Jen stood and went to the two discarded robes. Picking one up, along with the theatre keys, she drew the silk garment around her, jumped off the stage and skipped out of the auditorium. Once in the reception of the small theatre, she put the key in the door and locked it, before turning on her heels and almost running back to the stage. 'Now,' she said, as she climbed back onto the boards, 'we won't be interrupted. So important for the creative process, I find!'

'Oh, I agree totally!' giggled Rachel, who was now lying back on the bed, her long brown hair spread around her on the pillow, her face still flushed from her orgasm. 'So how are we going to play this scene?'

'Let's take it from when we're on the bed together?' Jen undid her robe and let it fall. Rachel smiled as she approached, and sat up as she climbed on alongside her. She got to her knees and slid her arms around Jen, who was also kneeling. Jen followed suit and their mouths collided in a kiss as passionate as the one they had shared at that first audition.

As they kissed Jen's hands wandered all over Rachel. She fondled her breasts, flicking the hard nipples. She squeezed her bottom, marvelling at its tightness. She placed a hand on each of her hips, revelling in the tapered waist, feeling it flaring out to become shapely hips and bottom. Finally, with trembling fingers, she touched Rachel's sex. Rachel twitched as Jen's fingertips tickled her pubic hair, but she also deepened the kiss, telling Jen that her desire would be returned.

As their tongues met, Jen eased a fingertip between Rachel's labia. It was hot and slick from her climax. Rachel's hips bucked forward, her body demanding more of Jen's finger. Jen obliged, pushing her index finger slowly into Rachel's pussy. She could feel Rachel's flesh sucking it in, and gave it a little wiggle. Rachel moaned and her arms tightened their grip around Jen's shoulders.

Finally the women broke their kiss. They looked into one another's eyes. 'I think my character would do this next,' said Jen, her voice throaty. Taking her arms from around Rachel, she pushed her gently back onto the bed. Rachel allowed herself to fall, her head landing softly on the pillow, her large breasts falling slightly either side of her ribs. Instinctively she opened her legs.

Jen loomed over her on all fours. She bent to kiss her again on the lips, and then ran her mouth down one side of her neck, delivering tiny little pecks as she went. She travelled across the upper slopes of Rachel's breasts until she reached her nipples. Sucking one of them deep inside her mouth, Jen felt the hard bud against her tongue. Flicking it, she squeezed the flesh below it with both hands. Rachel groaned. Switching her attention to the other breast, Jen gave it the same treatment, making Rachel writhe against the bed.

Lifting her head, Jen pushed Rachel's breasts together,

watching the cherry-red nipples bulge before releasing them. She resumed her trail of kisses down Rachel's body, opening her mouth slightly and allowing her tongue to trail over her co-star's smooth skin. Very soon she was at the apex of Rachel's thighs. She could smell her arousal.

Placing her fingers either side of Rachel's puffed-out lips, Jen looked into the depths of her sex. The tunnel of soft pink flesh suddenly seemed inviting, her neatly trimmed brown pubes framing her entrance perfectly. Jen took a deep breath and bent her head to kiss Rachel's cunt.

The first thing which struck her was the smell, a deep earthy aroma which drew her in further. Then there was the taste. It was raw and unscented, but it aroused something animal inside Jen, making her want more. Finally there was the feel of her tender flesh, its heat palpable on her tongue. The hairs at the top of her slit tickled the tip of her nose as she pointed her tongue and directed further inside Rachel.

Pushing her thumbs inside Rachel, hearing her gasp as she did so, she gently pulled the flower apart. Running her tongue up and down the exposed flesh, Jen warmed to her task. She began to use her lips as well, sucking as much of Rachel's sex into her mouth as she could. She felt Rachel's hands on her head, her legs over her shoulders, as she drove her on to another orgasm.

Suddenly Rachel was pushing herself up from the bed. 'Jen!' she called, 'Jen! Spin around!'

'W–what?' slurred Jen, reluctantly breaking away from Rachel's sex and looking up between her thighs.

'Spin around and give me your pussy! I want to eat you!' As Jen looked reluctant to move, Rachel added, 'I think our characters would "69"!'

Clambering around on the bed, Jen parted her thighs and lowered her groin onto Rachel's waiting mouth. She shuddered as they made contact, Rachel's fingers prying her apart, her mouth sucking at the exposed inner labia. Then her tongue pierced her, the way she had pierced Rachel, and a flick across her clit sent a jolt of lust through her.

Pulling herself together, she looked back at Rachel's pussy, now upside-down. Seizing her thighs in a tight grip, she pulled her legs further apart, and bent back to her task. She ran her tongue roughly down the length of Rachel's lips, and sucked at them hungrily. At the same time she felt Rachel's mouth doing much the same to her, her clit swelling and pulsing as her excitement was stoked by some of the most talented oral sex she had ever received.

'Mmmmm! Oh, yesssss!' Rachel screamed, tearing her mouth away from Jen, her orgasm about to burst. Jen was not going to be denied her own pleasure. Without breaking contact, she pushed her bottom back, forcing herself onto Rachel's mouth. Rachel's screams were muffled, as she took a mouthful of Jen and began to suck and lick her again.

Rachel started to slam against Jen's mouth in violent pumping movements. Suddenly her cunt began to pulse and was pressed hard onto her lips. A long low moan came from somewhere between Jen's own thighs, and Rachel's legs straightened and her toes curled. She had come again.

Jen's own clit was sending alarm signals through her body. Rachel was a considerate lover, stopping only for a few seconds, as her orgasm coursed through her. Jen felt firm hands gripping her buttocks, long nails scratching the flesh, as her bottom was pulled apart and a busy tongue flicked her button as hard as it could. Jen could feel the crisis growing. Throwing her head back, she howled in ecstasy, her stomach pumping in and out as she came on Rachel's face.

Jen collapsed forward, her cheek resting against Rachel's smooth thigh. She drifted off into another world, and was only vaguely aware of Rachel moving from underneath her and coming to lie beside her, arms around her, one palm resting gently on a breast, her belly nestled against her bottom.

The naked women lay that way for some time, until Jen stirred. Turning to look at Rachel, she gently kissed her awake. Rachel smiled, her beautiful brown eyes dancing with affection. 'Yes, I think that's what our characters would do!' she said, as both actresses started to giggle.

Claude was amazed at their progress at the next rehearsal. When the play opened the producer was delighted to find he really did have a hit on his hands. The controversial subject and explicit sex and nudity got the audiences in, but they left raving about the intense performances and raw energy of the two actresses, and their amazing chemistry. But although some speculated, Jen and Rachel never let on about their unique approach to method acting.

Kinky Girls

Women who act on their most shameful fantasies and embark upon the most daring misbehaviour, is still the most enduring and timeless theme in erotic fantasy, and loved by male and female readers alike. And this collection takes the idea of a kinky adventurous woman to the max. A collection of 20 original, varied, outrageous, eye-watering and utterly sensuous stories from the best new voices and established authors around today.

ISBN 9781907016561 £7.99

GIRL FUN 1
Adventures in Lesbian Loving
Edited by Miranda Forbes

Who needs boys when you can have **Girl Fun**?

Soft lips on smooth, supple skin, slender curves interlocking. No wonder girl-on-girl action has never been more popular.

Twenty tales of lip-smacking lesbian action guaranteed to make your next night out with the girls even more fun.

ISBN 9781906373672   £7.99